The Last Romantics

A novel

by

Elizabeth Malin

This book is a work of fiction. Characters and places are either made up or, if real, used fictitiously. Any resemblance between fictional characters and real people is entirely coincidental and not intentional.

———————————————

Publication date: November 2015

Visit the author's website for other books: young adult, historical, contemporary romance and more.

www.LibbyMalin.com

And consider leaving a review at book blogs and retail websites!

———————————————

Turn around,
Whirl and spin, lover,
Dance to me!
Take my hand, lover,
One step, and then another
Until eternity.
        — Ambrose Thomas D'Ispahan

CHAPTER ONE

MOST OF ALL, I wanted them to be happy. In the past few years, this wish has focused almost exclusively on her — she with the perfect lips and Arden face, the honey-gold hair that clouded around those rosebud cheeks, the tight little girl's body and the slim ankles. How could you not love her, especially when she was androgynous as Puck, sensual as Venus?

It was easy to assume that all their unhappiness originated with him, so self-absorbed, such an artiste, so cruelly ambivalent to her deepest yearnings. And then, of course, there was that other woman, in whose arms he sought comfort in the sunset of his too-short life.

Oh, there was a time when I despised him, when I believed all his fortune was undeserved, and all his misfortune brought on himself by his reckless disregard for those who loved him. But that followed the time when I thought he made the world spin with his tales of love and reckless girls who broke men's hearts.

As years went by…and stories unfolded, page after page of stories…one saw the entire tale. They were as ordinary as any folk, despite his gussying up their stories with drama and light. They loved. They fought. They irritated each other in the small ways we all do when the idea of something gets populated with the reality of it, the scent and sound and feel of it. Their ideas were harder than most to live up to, too, since he'd done such a fine job of making them shimmer and dance. The march of time has a way of dulling the glow. They couldn't help that.

There were no saints here. And since her happiness was so entwined with his, one had to wish they'd both just get on with it and decide they'd order a dish of it to share.

So few have that chance. Why couldn't they?

The corners on the papers in her lap ruffled in the breeze, struggling to fly away. She should go in. But she'd wanted to catch at least some of the March warmth on her shoulders while it lasted. It would be gone soon enough.

She shivered. The air was bright, the sky blue, but the grass beneath the old swing in the yard was brown and icy. Wispy X-ray image clouds portended the return of cold air. Easter was coming soon, yet she knew no one would be dressed in spring finery, and there was a chance of snow flurries in the forecast. Ah, Vermont.

She wanted to move. South, back below the Mason-Dixon line, where spring meant teasing warm days followed by cool, dreary ones, the season winking at you with impish delight, forcing a smile to your lips even as you raised your fist to cloud-dampened heavens. People smiled at you there, for no reason, said hello, nodded in acknowledgement of your existence.

The first year Kate and Jim lived in Vermont, she'd always been wondering if she'd done something wrong. Had she said something rude to the book store owner to cause him to look so dour? Taken too long at the library counter to have the librarian seem so grim? Placed sixteen items in the fifteen-item lane at the grocery store to cause the cashier to scowl? No "how you doin', hon?" here. No, "you have a good day, ya hear?" Just stony stares until business was transacted. Taciturn New England.

She snapped a rubber band around the pages and got off of the garden swing. Jim had put it in for her, and she'd hardly used it. The joke, "there are two seasons in Vermont, winter and the Fourth of July," turned out to be no joke. Jim loved it. Loved the cold, the skiing, the endless, cocooning snow. And for a long while, she'd loved it, too. Loved the sense of settling in when the first flakes began to fall in late November. Loved the soft hush of the snow followed by the comforting crunch of the plows up and down, up and down the town roads. Loved the safety—she didn't even know where her house key was anymore—the solitude, the sense of escape. And, yes, the soaring mountains that turned a velvet green she couldn't adequately describe in summer, the brilliant hues that painted them in autumn, an autumn that began the last weeks of August.

The problem with escape was that, after a while, you felt marooned in your pod of security, like a castaway, and you realized that refuge meant being a refugee, never quite here, always longing to be…there.

"Jim?" she called as she approached the house, yawning. Her eyes were tired, and her shoulders ached.

The sun might not have warmed her body, but it had dimmed her vision. She took a moment to adjust to the shadows of the kitchen and was about to call his name again, when she heard his iPod downstairs in the basement.

Just one more year and then you'd be happy

"Baker Street." She heard him humming along as he worked.

No, not worked. Played. Mocked. He was painting again, he, who had no training in art, who'd decided that abstract expressionism meant he could wear the moniker artist, just like she did.

Except she didn't really wear it yet, did she? She was a romance novelist striving to be taken seriously, trying to sell a...a what? An "upmarket" novel. She couldn't even bring herself to say "literary fiction." People like her didn't write literary fiction, gals who'd gone to community college, been raised in unfashionable suburbs, had set tables with the fork on the right just as her mother had for many years, and thought until recently that you pronounced posthumously *post-hyue-muss-ly*. Girls with maiden names like Brznecki, married names like Lazlo. She wrote under the name Kate Landon.

No, *literary* writers went to Princeton or Yale or some prestigious writing program. They read the *New Yorker* regularly and knew about the *Paris Review*. They praised the latest literary wonders, no matter how empty their works seemed to her. She had no code to decipher that language. They were on the inside. She was always peering in.

She placed the yellowed papers on the kitchen island, wondering what to do about dinner, resentment creeping in to her thoughts. She wanted Jim to think of these things when she was immersed in writing projects. He would if she asked. She just didn't want to have to ask.

Grimacing, she strode to the basement door, opened it and called down to him.

"Are you hungry?" she yelled over the music.

"Not really," he called back up to her.

Great. If he wasn't hungry, then she was definitely in charge of dinner. After walking back to the fridge, she grabbed some celery and carrot sticks to munch on while she perused the possibilities. Nothing triggered her culinary imagination. She'd hoped he would have stopped at the store to pick up a few things when he was out—she assumed he was out earlier when she'd been writing. But if she didn't specifically tell him to get something, he just got what was on his mind and nothing else. Then he'd snap at her for reminding him of the lapse—why didn't you tell me, he'd say.

Not really hungry? she thought to herself. *Fine, then, starve along with me.*

Lately, she often found herself irritated with Jim, the smallest things setting her off. And the unthinkable *had* started to creep into her thinking. Maybe she should just move out of Vermont...alone. Would he follow? Would it matter? Where would she go—who would she become?

She didn't know anymore who Kate was, only Kate-and-Jim.

She thought of going to the basement and insisting he handle dinner, telling him that she was going to write until it was time to eat, and then stalking back to her office. Instead, she grabbed the Rutherford papers and headed to her lair without saying anything, letting her slamming door speak for her.

❧

THE MARCH OF TIME by Beatrice Rutherford

By fortune and misfortune, I was born in the South, two years shy of the century mark, two years younger than he was, two years older than her.

Poverty wasn't a word we used in our household. We just made do on acreage that had been in the family for a century, worked once by slaves, then by sharecroppers. Daddy wasn't a mean boss, but he expected his rents on time. He had bills to pay, too.

One brother, Henry, went off to Montgomery — yes, her city, though I didn't find out until later we'd been virtually neighbors all those years ago — getting a job as a banker because he was good with numbers. Another brother, Earl, not liking the farming or the landlord life much either, headed for New Orleans where he made a lot of money that Momma refused to talk about. He ran some whorehouses was my best guess. They're all gone now, and I shake my head with regret thinking of how little I did to stay in touch over the years.

Back then, I was headed for the things most of the other girls in my neck of the woods had their eyes on — marriage, family, years of just living — when three events happened that twisted that course for me.

First, there was Jeremy Lynn Rutherford, III, a preacher's son who came through our town to pay a visit on our own minister and stayed a bit, ending up courting and marrying me. So far, this was what I'd expected of life.

I best not write a lot about Jeremy. To this day, I love him still, love the great height of him — over six feet — and the long mouth that could hardly do anything but smile, and big shock of red-brown hair and the green-brown eyes that always seemed to be hiding some joke. I think one of the reasons I fell so hard later in life for *him* was because of how Jeremy made me feel and how it seemed to me *he* had captured that first-love feeling so well in all his books, that sense that you'll never trod that path again no matter who you meet or how he makes you feel.

But the second thing that came along stole Jeremy from me. Just a year after we married, he went off to the War and didn't come back. By then, I'd had our babe and lost him—infantile, the doctor said, but it could have been any of a dozen fevers back then—and was settling in to whatever life had yet to throw at me when...

The third thing happened. I sometimes played organ and sang in church, and the fourth Sunday of Easter, I set to wailing out "Leaning" or "How Great Thou Art"—the specific hymn now escapes me—when some fellow comes up to me after church raving about my voice and telling me I should "study" and sing on the stage. Why, that was like saying I should go work with my brother in New Orleans. Singing on the stage wasn't a refined line of work in my family. But, no, he said he was talking about something of a higher nature. The high arts, that is. Opera. Recitals. Real music by real fine composers.

Folks had always told me I sang like a bird, but I'd never thought about doing anything grand with it. I already had a little music training, the piano and organ lessons that allowed me to help out at church services now and again. And I'd figured after marriage and children, I might even contribute to the family income by offering a few piano lessons to little ones.

But after Jeremy's passing, and baby's, too, I felt free to use it for other callings. I felt free to leave. That's what those deaths did for me. They uprooted me. I'd been feeling a melancholy yearning for a time after my sorrow had passed in full, and had just attributed it to natural grieving, the type that never leaves you. But this visitor, he made my heart leap at the prospect of doing something different, and the contrast in how I'd felt before that suggestion to how I felt after it taught me my melancholy had a remedy. At least a palliation. So I had the courage and strength of will to listen to this man—a music teacher, Mr. Flockstone, from Atlanta in town visiting his grandparents—and evaluate for myself whether what he said had meaning.

It did and he did. He didn't give up, came round the next day, offered to pay my way to Atlanta to study in his school. Momma was skeptical, Daddy opposed. But I was ready to face what this new freedom offered, even though I suspected in my heart of hearts that this man was something of an artist, all right, but maybe leaning a little to the confidence side of the definition.

It turned out he was both. Yes, he had a music school, a little thing in a run-down building, and he knew music. He taught me aria after aria, practically swooning over my ability to memorize quickly, and he commenced trying to seduce me.

If I'd not been married previously, I might have fallen for his flattery and un-subtle physicalities, the hand lingering over mine, his breath on my neck as he peered over my shoulders, his hands encircling my waist to make a point about breathing right. Being familiar with man-woman intimacies and the mating dance itself, however, I was fully aware of where his attention seemed to be leading. It flattered me. I'd been traveling in a desert long enough to enjoy the complimentary patter he showered on me. It sent a thrill through me, I admit, even if I never for a second considered straying with this particular gentleman. But he reminded me of something important — I wasn't unattractive. I had a shapely body and lustrous dark hair and a face akin to a famous cinematic star, or so my Jeremy had sworn. It was nice to be thus reminded.

When he tried to kiss me after what he called a "rapturous rendition" of *"Visi d'arte,"* I ended things and told him I'd find a teacher elsewhere, thank you kindly. I chided myself for leading him on just to salve my womanly ego.

My money was nearly spent by then — I'd only had a little left over from Jeremy's insurance, and I'd used it on lodging and food, sparingly, yes, but I had to eat.

I had enough for a train ticket, by golly, and a little left over after that for maybe a month's board...in New York.

Mr. Flockstone had told me I should head to the city. He'd told me I should audition for the Metropolitan Opera. He'd told me, too, of a teacher he respected there, a Madame Solinsky.

Having pulled myself up from the Alabama soil already, I had no problem flinging my future at this unknown Solinsky and a career — or not — with any opera company. I was of a mind to try things. I knew life was happening out there somewhere. I'd had a small taste of it in Atlanta. I knew that whatever I thought my future would have been with Jeremy was as dead and buried as he and our baby.

Mr. Flockstone and that whole Atlanta experience had refreshed my memory of what it meant to be alive and even alluring, to be...a woman.

I was new and fresh and, I was sure, able to weather any disappointments that came my way. After experiencing what I'd already suffered, you can understand my naivete. I thought I'd been to the bottom already.

So I moved to New York. And that's where I met, and fell under the spell of *him*.

CHAPTER TWO

WAS THE *HIM* in *The March of Time* F. Scott Fitzgerald? The writer, a woman identified as "Beatrice Rutherford," didn't say at first, and Kate had only just begun reading.

At least Kate had this from Jim—these papers had been in an old trunk he'd insisted on buying on a trip to North Carolina early in the month, a trip they couldn't really afford but decided to take anyway after a particularly happy visit home, first to her sister and then on to his folks in New Jersey on the way back north. He'd known how she missed the warmth of spring, so he'd surprised her and taken her farther south to catch more of it, as if she could stash it away in her luggage to comfort her when they went to the icy north again. He'd seen the trunk in a used-furniture shop. It had only cost twenty dollars. And he'd wanted it to store his things in, his paints, his brushes, his rags.

At home, he'd set about cleaning it and found, in a secret drawer, a sheaf of pages, some typed, some handwritten, tied together under a single sheet that had "The March of Time, My Memoir by Beatrice Rutherford" scrawled on it.

She'd thought of going back to college, for the graduate degree she realized was the true passport to a different career. Maybe in English. The Rutherford papers might help her there. Maybe she could teach somewhere...at a college. She'd like that, being on a peaceful campus, surrounded by quiet learners. She'd approached some colleges in the area about offering workshops in writing commercial fiction but had been rebuffed. Who was she with her silly romance novels, nearly ten years of writing now...but it amounted to nothing to them. Jim had been angry for her, denouncing them as "the academic one-percenters." Half the world reads romance, he'd fumed, and she'd smiled at his feminism. Half the world.

But still she'd cherished the hope that one day, some campus would welcome her. And if it took a graduate degree....

She could write a paper about the Rutherford memoir. If it was Scott this Beatrice Rutherford was writing about...colleges would clamor to have a piece of this, and she'd make sure they accepted her with the package.

"Your editor called while I was on the phone." Jim startled her. She'd not heard him come up or open the door. He turned, and she could see him retrieve a beer from the fridge and look back at her. He looked tired. And dirty. His torn T-shirt was splattered with paint and grease stains. A shock of thick brown hair cut across his forehead, stubble bloomed on his angular face. Tall and lanky when she'd met him, he now had a fuller, more muscular look, not from working out but from physically working. He did every repair on their old house himself, and he plowed the snow off their drive in the winter manually. He skied whenever he could, and he took walks in the nearby forests during good weather—avoiding hunting season.

"Did you change the oil?" she asked him.

"How could I do that—you had the car earlier."

She'd meant, had he changed it earlier, before she'd run errands—his shirt looked as though he had, and she'd not seen him since she'd gone to the bank and returned. She let it go.

"Did she say what she wanted—why didn't you come get me?" Kate neatened her files in the small room on the back of the house facing the yard and carefully put Beatrice Rutherford's papers on her desk, next to the computer.

"Something about your proposal—that she wants to talk about it." He leaned against the doorjamb, and damned if she didn't find herself admiring him, wanting him. Whatever their troubles over the years, the "physicalities" of marriage weren't among them. "Your door was shut. Thought you were working."

A ball formed in Kate's stomach, born of anger and frustration. Jim should have interrupted her. How passive-aggressive. He'd honored her dictate not to disturb her when writing, yes, but he must have known she'd have wanted to take a call from her editor.

So, Alice wanted to talk about her proposal. That didn't sound good. She'd been churning out romances for more than fifteen years, each one following the next seamlessly, fan letters and emails making her glow with satisfaction, but lately...in the past couple years, things had changed. Her hand on the phone, she looked at Jim, sending the silent message he should leave. He took the hint, and she immediately punched in her editor's number, relieved when it didn't get tossed to voice mail.

"Alice, Jim said you called?" Kate said. She didn't identify herself—no need. She'd had a relationship with Alice for ten years now, never having moved beyond her original publisher, deals negotiated by a series of agents. She was without one now, having ended her last agent relationship when she'd figured out that she spent more time scrutinizing her contracts than the agent did. Besides, that agent had not been interested in anything Kate wrote outside of romance. It sat on her desk unread, or she said she just "didn't get it."

"Thanks for getting back to me so quickly!" Alice's smooth voice oozed over the line. She'd always been supportive of Kate's writing, even complimenting her profusely when asking for changes. "I've been looking over this proposal for the next book—the Scottish trilogy—and you know I think this is a fabulous idea, Scottish historicals are selling really well, and I think you'll find a whole new fan base there, but…it seems a bit tame, dear. I'm wondering if there's a way we can heat it up a bit."

Kate's heart dropped. This wasn't the first time Alice had suggested this. She'd asked for more "sizzle" or "heat" or "steam" or "passion" in virtually every conversation they'd had about the past three books she'd written. What she really meant was: sex. She wanted Kate to write sex scenes, and in Kate's books, intimacy occurred off screen.

The book industry had been roiled by changes recently, most notably the digital revolution, but there had also been a quieter tide flowing through genre fiction, or rather, her particular genre. Ever since several red-hot romances had hit the best seller charts, some of them self-published, erotica seemed to be the ticket to success. Her own publisher's romance imprint had gone two years without a best seller, a first for them, and she knew her editor was feeling the pressure. They'd just started their own erotica imprint, called "Climax."

"My readers might be turned off by that. I mean, I'm afraid I'd lose some of them," Kate said weakly, feeling tired. She'd said it before. This wasn't a sense of déjà vu she was feeling. It was true repetition. Alice argued for more sex, Kate demurred, but eventually threw in some lines here and there about his "taut abs" or "tight manhood," or her "wet heat" or "pounding desire," and things went on as before. She was well aware of Alice's desire for her to heat up the pages more, but she'd figured her new proposal, set in popular Scottish highlands with kilt-wearing warriors, would be a slam-dunk even without the sex. She'd not expected any push-back beyond a few suggestions here and there.

"Mmm, I think it's more likely readers will expect it. You're going to have to stretch yourself a little, Kate. And you know what? I think you'll be great at it!"

Stretch herself? Kate knew what that meant. "Taut abs" and "tight manhood" weren't enough. This was more ominous. She was beginning to realize that the sex—or lack of it—could be a deal breaker.

"Your readership is changing, sweetie. Your numbers indicate that, well, to be frank, you're losing some readers already. And I don't want that to happen. I love you—you know that. I don't want to lose you. I want new readers to find you and appreciate your amazing talent."

Kate's face warmed as her hands turned clammy. "Don't want to lose you"—that was the closest Alice had ever come to suggesting her next book might not be accepted. What would Kate do without that advance? She and Jim needed it to pay the bills. They'd stopped working "regular" jobs once the advance checks had started rolling in year after year. She had to sell this book, and the next one and the next one. Should she try another publishing house? She'd need a new agent for that, and she'd procrastinated on getting one, because she really wanted to sell a different kind of book entirely, something people would remember. Should she self-publish? The mountain of work required made her heart sink. The research, the learning curve...

"I think you're overthinking it," Alice went on. "It's really not so big in the scheme of things. We're all adults here. Do you get what I'm saying?"

"Yes, I do understand, Alice. It's just that...I'd had this idea that Ramona was an innocent and—"

"Well, that's perfect. The virginal heroine, and the hero introduces her to the pleasures of true love. It gives me chills thinking about it. I've made some marks on the proposal, places where I think you can easily amp up the physical attraction between Ramona and Owen, just little things...I think if you look it over, you'll not find it difficult to imagine at all. You're such a good writer, Kate, with such a great creative way with descriptions. I know you can do it. And I think you'll enjoy doing it."

Kate was pretty sure she wouldn't enjoy it. She felt a stubborn resistance to it, in fact. It wasn't that she was a prude. In real life, she and Jim could certainly heat up the sheets. And she regularly read a couple romance novelists who wrote incredibly steamy material in suspense and fantasy, and she admired and enjoyed them. She just thought it was unnecessary for her material, an easy way to signal attraction between a couple—throw in the lust. She wanted people to take her seriously as a writer and was working hard to achieve that goal. This pushed it farther away.

"Maybe I should go back to contemporary," she murmured, thinking of scrapping the historical romance idea to return to the sweet romances that had begun her career. Historical required so much research, and although she'd already done a fair share for the new Scottish trilogy idea, writing contemporary required nothing more than knowing how to describe the current fashions.

"Do you have any ideas?" Alice sounded excited.

Ouch—that was too quick. Had Alice called to tell her she was rejecting the Ramona story, only giving Kate this last chance to make it right? Panic fueled anger. She knew her readers were out there—what was the publishing company doing to help her find them? Wasn't that their job? Weren't they supposed to do more than just print the damn book and truck it to bookstores? She wondered for the umpteenth time if she should go it alone, joining the ranks of authors who'd self-published digitally and had great success. She had a fan base. She could try it. Maybe get her rights reverted back and even offer her back list for sale—no, too messy. Would take a team of lawyers to get her publisher to admit her books were officially "out of print." Damned bloodsuckers. For years, she'd felt immensely grateful to her publisher for allowing her to tell her stories. Lately, she'd felt more and more resentful, more and more used.

Frustrated, she snapped, "Yeah, how's this? Strangers meet on a train. Have a hot and heavy one-night stand a la *Last Tango in Paris*...on a train...a moving train...lots of Freudian imagery there, hulking train, plunging into the dark...and...and the two meet again five years later, connection still a live wire and—"

"I'm liking it!"

But she hadn't been serious. She hadn't meant....inwardly, she growled as she listened to Alice prattle on about plot possibilities, virtually all of them impossible to write without huge story problems.

By the time they were finished, she realized with despair that she now had to write this book. Or sex up her Ramona/Owen idea. But she couldn't bring herself to change that vision. Maybe if she landed a new agent, he or she would sell the Scottish trilogy to another publisher.

With a groan, she sat at her computer and began typing, but not a story, emails to her two novelist friends, Marie and Jacqueline. While Jim had a few guys in town he occasionally got together with to ski or watch a game, Kate's best friends were far away. Both were published, like her, in romance. Marie wrote fantasy, Jackie young adult. They'd met at a Romance Writers of America conference five years ago and had corresponded ever since even though they both lived in Illinois and Kate in Vermont.

Within a few moments of firing off her tale to them, Marie sent back a reply: *At least she didn't ask for vampires. Or did she?*

Jacqueline's reply came in immediately after that: *Or zombies. Or Fifty Shades of Vampire Zombies featuring a wizard boy named Larry Dotter. Or Twilight. Or grief porn. Grief porn is really big right now. I'm thinking of penning a book about a paraplegic amputee teen gal who falls in love with an orphaned Stephen Hawking-type guy whose only remaining adult relative has a heart attack and dies in front of him and he can't do anything, so he's racked with guilt – or maybe wracked by guilt, the copy editor will fix that – but anyway then one of our pair gets…bad news.*

Kate: *Gawd, what could be worse than all that?*

Marie: *They're…brother and sister?*

Jackie: *Haven't made up my mind on the terminal illness yet. Or its victim. Hmm…maybe…both?*

Kate: *I thought the erstwhile lovers in grief porn had to be purty.*

Marie: *True that.*

Jackie: *Damn. I was so close.*

Kate: *Just get rid of the disabilities.*

Marie: *Yeah, the heart attack/ guilt thing is still a nice touch.*

Jackie: *But then he could have, you know, called 911.*

Kate: *Tie him up.*

Marie: *Have him do drugs. He's wiped when the beloved aunt drops.*

Kate: *"Her blank blue eyes aimed like a laser into his heart, shattering him and his future. Oh, God, what had he done?!"*

Marie: *Yeah, a juvie.*

Kate: *Saved by lurv....*

Jackie: *Luv with a capital L. Grief porn is always love with a capital L.*

Marie: *Grief porn is all eros and no psyche — no insight into how the tragedy might be transformed into something else. It makes you wonder what the point is, and what it says about our culture that this stuff is so popular.*

Jackie: *Uh, that was...deep.*

Marie: *Sorry, I've been doing a lot of reading about Shakespeare, thinking of setting a time travel in that period, and I got sidetracked reading about drama and melodrama.*

Kate: *No need to apologize. You schooled me real good.*

Kate also learned that Jackie's editor was asking for a slew of revisions to her latest work, a complex teen story of elves and dragons: *She wants me to have my hero slay a dragon in the first chapter. Uh, the whole point of the book is that he has to slay it to prove his valor to the heroine's father in order to win her hand. If I do it in the first chapter, the story's kind of over.*

Kate shot back: *Ouch. What are you going to do? Did you tell her that?*

Marie: *I never assume an editor's revision notes are to be taken literally. Had too many revisions to the revisions and learned my lesson. Their revision notes are a code. You just need to decode what's bugging the editor, and then fix that problem your own way. She wants my hero to be more heroic from the get-go. I can do that.*

And from Jackie: *My editor told me to make my hero more sympathetic. I gave him a dog. And a British accent.*

More from Marie: *Hey, you guys know that fellow John Jackson, the one who writes all those novelizations of television shows? He's got some screed up on his blog against fan fiction writers.*

Kate: *Uh, isn't he kind of paid to write fan fiction?*

Jackie: *Some of my best friends are fan fiction writers.* ☺

Marie: *He writes all kinds of advice to writers about writing and publishing. In a nutshell – I'm so special and you're all plebeians put on this earth to admire me, so give it up now. Oh, and self-publishing = loser.*

Jackie: *Self-publishing is the future!*

Marie: *If you're in the right genre. Like erotica. Sells like hottie-cakes.*

Kate: *As I know all too well. Gotta go write my own hottie-cakes now....*

The Last Romantics

CHAPTER THREE

WISHFUL THINKING--PROLOGUE
Lust with a capital L. A train piercing the night, its gray-noise horn a throbbing echo of Jake Blaine's inner ache. A beautiful woman. Candles twinkling in the club car. A glass of wine. He was lonely. That was all. Lonely.

She stared over her wineglass at him, taking the time to study his features as he sat down with his own drink. What did she see? He was tall, rugged face, blondish hair, blue eyes that one woman had told him held "pain as well as mirth." Not necessarily the dark, handsome type. But virile enough. She'd said he made her feel safe.

She'd liked his British accent. Observant—it was nearly gone now. He'd moved to America as a child with his parents, and felt a true-blue Yank. Women's attraction to the British accent annoyed him most of the time. It seemed shallow. Not so with her. She was refreshingly frank, acknowledging outright that the whole Brit appeal was a "fangirl" thing she usually resisted. Usually.

She gave her head the slightest of shakes, as if trying to rattle some sense back into it. She said she "wasn't that kind of gal." The kind to meet with a strange man on a train.

"Here we go," he said amiably, holding up his glass. "A toast. To clumsiness."

Ever since she'd boarded in Chicago, she'd been running into him. Literally. They'd nearly collided when she'd stepped onto the train, then they'd crossed paths in the corridor, laughing as they bumped into each other. "This is getting to be a habit," he'd said good-naturedly, and then offered to carry her bag. And, they'd been seated together in the dining car that evening, sharing a delightful meal and conversation, and laughter over her spilled wineglass. Which had led to him asking her to join him for a drink to make up for it.

She was returning home to California from her sister Rosemary's wedding in Maryland which had left her joyful and a little blue, too, she'd confided. Rosemary was so in love, so happy, whereas Belinda was still…searching. He let her talk. He had his own searches going on, paralleling hers.

She looked at him as they sat in the twilight-infused club car like old friends while the train made its relentless way west, throbbing with power and jostling them against each other. Seated close enough together that their knees touched, she didn't pull away. If anything, she seemed to press farther in. She'd smiled at his gestures of civility, thanked him.

Something about her spoke to him. A vulnerability she tried to mask. A hunger. It matched his own, a gnawing hunger for…more.

Jake Blaine did not believe in love at first sight. In fact, he didn't believe in a lot of things unless he had the numbers to prove it. He was a cautious, meticulous man who spent the majority of his time counseling people against wishful thinking. It was his job. He was a polling company CEO, one of the best in the business, sought after by candidates, advocacy organizations, political parties – anyone who wanted to put their finger on the pulse of the people.

Jake had been in the business long enough, in fact, to use its techniques to evaluate personal matters. Like this one. He had been on the Golden Zephyr train since last night, heading cross-country to California for a consulting job. The trip would take longer, but it was one of the things he'd promised himself and his younger brother this year—that he'd slow down, "smell the roses," do things he enjoyed. And he'd always wanted to cross the country by train.

The first time he'd passed her in the train corridor, she had smiled. He'd given himself a forty percent favorable rating with that smile.

The next time they had bumped into each other, she had giggled. Probably over the magic fifty percent and gaining on sixty.

When they'd ended up at a table together in the dining car, his favorability ratings were going off the chart, if her smile, gestures, conversation and general…electricity…were any indication.

It turned out that Ms. Belinda Remington – of the raven-colored hair and seductive widow's peak, the heart-shaped face and brown-green eyes, the cream complexion and Clara Bow lips – hated flying.

"I'm headed home," she'd said over a glass of Merlot at dinner.

Her smile had warmed him. He'd not been in a serious relationship for a time, and his brother kept urging him to date more. He had to admit he was getting to that age where striving and achieving didn't satisfy as they once did, creating a fear that nothing ever would. Had he missed something important in life? God, he wasn't even forty, not ancient. Yet sometimes, he felt like the oldest man alive. Tired.

Tired of tough talkers and hard-shelled businesspeople. Not that he was interested in phony compassion or Mother Teresa wannabes. He just craved…honesty. Belinda offered it, a refreshing unembarrassed brightness about her phobia, about herself, as if she expected tenderness because that's what she'd offer in return. He realized as she talked just how tired he was of the "sophisticated" set he ran with, educated, cultured, well-to-do people who might be there for him or any other friend in a pinch but who presented a cool aloofness to the world, as if afraid to be viewed as soft. It wearied him. Belinda, by contrast, was self-confident and educated, but not…hard. "How about you?"

"Actually, I live in the East," he had said at dinner. "I'm going west for a consulting job."

"Oh. Where?"

"San Francisco."

"Really? I live around Monterey, about two hours away," she'd said. The train had rattled suddenly, sending her wineglass spilling. "Oh, dear," she'd said, reaching for her napkin to mop up the mess. Jake had done the same, and for an instant, their hands had crossed. He'd felt like pulling her close. She'd looked up at him and cocked her head to one side, her eyes opening wide, little rose petals of blush on her cheeks. Yes, she'd felt it, too.

"Let me buy you a drink to make up for that," he'd suggested.

"I thought you'd never ask," she'd responded.

Now, they were spending time in the club car, during which time he learned that she was twenty-four, she had graduated from Stanford just a couple years ago, where she had majored in communications and now worked as an assistant in a small public relations firm. While they talked, Jake found himself achingly aware that her presence aroused him. He felt his manhood tighten.

She wore snug blue jeans and a form-fitting white T-shirt. The club car was cool from air-conditioning. When she shivered in the cold air, he offered her his jacket. His fingers lingered on her shoulders when he draped his blue blazer over her arms. She did not protest. In fact, she reached up and held his hand on one shoulder for a second or two. He wasn't used to this. He could hardly speak. With great effort, he sat down.

Maybe he needed to be a little more spontaneous, to let the sparks fly.

Hell, sparks were sure to fly soon. When he looked over at Ms. Belinda Remington, his libido felt like a kite in a lightning storm.

She must have sensed it, too. She patted his hand, then didn't remove hers while they continued to converse.

"I know we've just met," Jake managed to say eventually. "But may I have your phone number and address? I travel quite a bit. Perhaps I could look you up."

She jumped at the chance. In fact, she stood quickly. "Come back to my compartment. I left my business cards there."

Business cards? Her compartment. It didn't take a rocket scientist—or a staid polling company executive—to figure out where she was really heading.

She made the first move, melting into his arms as soon as she opened the door, while he pushed up against her, kissing her deeply, her musky perfume intoxicating his senses, making his legs weaken as other places continued to strengthen, a hard knot of desire that made it difficult to breathe or do anything but press himself against her, feeling her pulsing desire in the throb of a vein in her throat.

"I don't normally do this sort of thing," he said between fiery kisses, his fingers trembling as they rubbed through her hair and down her back.

"Neither do I," she responded, her lips pliant, her body hot. Her fingers rubbed his waist, coming around to the front where she touched his heavy arousal.

He sucked in his breath. "Damn," he said softly.

"I'm not hurting you?" she asked, pulling her hand away.

"No, no, not at all," he said moving her hand back.

She then pulled off her shirt, revealing small, perfectly formed breasts held in by pink lace. He nuzzled at her chest while she unbuttoned his shirt and his belt buckle, running her hands across his abdomen and up his chest, her comments on his "taut abs" making him grateful he'd taken Chris's advice and joined a gym.

"There isn't much room," she said, pulling him to her bed.

"We can be creative," he said, reaching into his pocket for a foil-wrapped packet. His younger brother had insisted he take some with him. *Maybe you'll get lucky,* Christopher had said to him. *Lord knows you should try. It's been too long.*

There was no time to think about his brother's attempts to encourage Jake's love life. Belinda Remington was driving him to the brink by taking the condom from him. Her fingers on him drove him crazy. They both were crazy, he thought. They were insane. It must be the water. The train ride, its romanticism, its hypnotic movement forward, pushing and throbbing and penetrating the mountains and rills. It was a Freudian Siren Song, seducing them both.

He leaned into her, playing with her body, his fingers feeling her moist heat while she moaned with delight. She looked down at him and let out a shiver of anticipation. When he felt her begin to shudder against his touch, he pulled himself up, ready for what they both craved.

And that's when they derailed.

No one was injured, thank god, but Jake's shot at a hot one-night stand was gone.

CHAPTER FOUR

NOT STEAMY ENOUGH, she thought. This was like writing grief porn, except without the grief. Didn't they have the same goals — to titillate, arouse intense feelings?

From the kitchen, Jim called.

"Is there anything for dinner or you wanna get pizza?"

"For God's sake, just order something!" she yelled back. "I'm working." She could probably finish another chapter if she wrote for another hour — a rough draft, at least. She got up to close the door that was slightly ajar, but Jim appeared first.

"What's the matter?" he said, sounding angry himself.

"Nothing."

He heaved an annoyed sigh. "Right."

"Just take care of dinner. That's the deal." An unspoken deal. Once she'd become the major breadwinner with her writing, she'd expected Jim to pitch in more with household tasks. He'd stepped up and did most of the cleaning, but meal-planning was a constant source of irritation for her. He often left it til the last minute, if he did it at all, and she'd come out of her office after a long writing session, hungry and tired, to find the kitchen dirty and the stove cold.

"I have a lot to do," she continued. "And I don't have time to fix dinner."

"So we'll order out," he said, his voice thin.

"Great. Just take care of it."

"Yes, ma'am," he said with mock respect and stomped back to the kitchen. She heard him call in the order, and she closed the door, grateful she'd set this boundary after her first book sale—when the door was closed, she wasn't to be disturbed. She was writing. Oh, how important it had made her feel, how authorly.

She rubbed her tired eyes and leaned against the door, feeling anything but authorly. She felt…petty. How could Jim make her feel that way without hurling an accusation? And why wouldn't he just take care of dinner instead of making such a big deal out of it?

Now she'd have to fight past her bad feelings to get any writing done. She went to the desk, stared at the words she'd just written, and sat, head in hands, waiting. Waiting for this mood to pass. Waiting to give up on being mad at Jim. Waiting.

She closed her eyes. She was so tired. Maybe she should turn on some music. No, Jim might have painted to music, but memories provided her background noise.

Random recollections floated through her mind when she wrote. Unrelated to the story she was penning or its characters, they were all happy moments or things that had delighted her. Now she remembered an autumn when she and Jim had first started seeing each other. It was his birthday, and they were going out to eat that evening at a fancy restaurant downtown. But she'd been unsure of how much time they'd have before heading there, so she'd worn her best little black dress all day, even when they'd gone hiking in the woods to catch some fall color. It had been warm that day, and she'd felt sweaty by the end of their amble. But it hadn't mattered because it was a special day, his birthday, and she was so eager to be with him that discomfort was eclipsed by their growing love.

It was as if writing had become a form of suspended animation. For the hours she sat at the computer, she was transfixed in time. In those moments, while the working part of her brain tapped out other characters' stories, she lived moments from her own story, moving smoothly from snapshot to mental snapshot, as if they were living tableaux:

A drive to her sister's house on a back road, turning a curve and going past an old white spired church, its graveyard nearby filled with thin, leaning slabs. The sky blue and bright. The air soft. The radio on. Something old. *You are the magnet and I am the steel.*

How that memory had filled her with longing to be home, to see her sister! And then she'd made the drive the next time she'd visited her sister, and it wasn't the same. The memory had been in slow motion, every nanosecond a flash of a camera frame as the curve appeared... then the church in bright afternoon light...then her head turned...then the graveyard landscape presented itself...

Writing was her amber, in which she preserved her life, little jots of it, bit by bit, tiny specs trapped in a warm glow. No reader would ever know what was really there, what was true.

She started writing at last, losing track of time. When she was too tired to be coherent any longer, she saved what she'd written so far, under the title "Wishful Thinking." Alice would like that.

With a great weariness, she pulled out a manila file marked "Spawn of Satan" and opened it. It was her latest agent research. She'd queried several already with another manuscript, a serious coming-of-age story, the only romance in it a secondary plot line. She tapped out a few more queries, throwing in that she had a proposal worked up for a sweet Scottish romance trilogy, too.

Kate had had three agents. The first had been a bully, aggressive with contract negotiations but also with her dealings with Kate, treating her questions and suggestions as if they came from an idiot. Kate had severed the relationship when Jim caught her crying after a phone conversation with her and pointed out the obvious — the agent worked for Kate, not the other way around.

The second agent had been too timid, a trait Kate realized she'd mistaken for kindness. Agent Two was supposed to help her land contracts outside of romance. But that agent was new at her craft and was constantly doing a "Mother, may I?" routine with the more experienced owner of the agency, causing delays in any submissions of her non-romance material. When submissions did occur, Kate learned they were little more than transmittal processes, no talking up of the manuscript, just query, cover letter and manuscript, and when rejections came in, the agent did nothing beyond passing them along to Kate.

In fact, Kate learned from Agent Three that some of those rejections might have been turned into resubmissions if Kate had done some manuscript tweaking. The problem with Agent Three wasn't that she lacked savvy or understanding. She had taken on too many clients. It took weeks for her to return an email or phone call. But she reassured Kate that she was always working for her, just not telling her everything she was doing. Turned out, she wasn't doing much beyond negotiating her contracts, which were pretty boilerplate by then anyway. When Kate discovered that her digital rights clause was worse than most, she pulled the plug. Hell, she could negotiate bad contracts on her own without giving away fifteen percent of the deal to a middleman.

When she'd first been published, Kate had thought she'd reached Nirvana, or at least a safe harbor. She'd thought, you sold to a publisher and then…your writing life began. And it had seemed that way for a long while, with book after book picked up by Alice, with a pile of glowing fan letters, with great reviews in romance publications and even one review in *Publishers Weekly* that had praised her "smart, elegant voice."

But the publishing world was no different than any other. Nothing was permanent; you had to succeed with every new "product." And past success didn't guarantee you respect from agents or even editors.

Respect was important to Kate, very important. Coming from a humble, no, an "unclassy" background, she always felt her mental dukes come up when she thought someone was looking down on her. As a writer, she could use words like puissant and insouciant and quotidian with confidence. But she didn't know how to pronounce them. She had grown up in a milieu—that, she knew how to say!—where that kind of vocabulary didn't enter conversation.

Around her fifth romance novel, she yearned to tell stories that weren't limited by the romance formula. She yearned to have heroines who were so flawed as to be almost unlikable, and heroes who sometimes had to find the heroic part of their nature before the story's end. She yearned, too, to write tales that didn't have a tidy ending. Oh, she would always hint at an HEA – happily ever after – but she wanted to pen stories where the reader supplied the ending, depending on her point of view about life.

It had taken her five years to actually write such a story, after making stabs at various un-romancey manuscripts over the years, finishing several that her agents hadn't marketed well, if at all. But now she felt like a new foal, trembling on unstable legs, making her way into the world as if she'd never been here before. Her new opus was tentatively called *Stillwater Dreams*, a coming of age story, maybe even a young adult, depending on how it was marketed, that probably qualified as a true *roman a clef*—a lot of her own early life was in it, her fears, her sense of not fitting in. And there was no hero, really, although plenty of friends and supporting characters.

She'd shared parts of it with Jim, but only parts. He liked it a lot, saw the difference in style, the maturity of her voice, the "elegance" of it, he'd said. He'd kissed her sweetly on the forehead after one reading, and said, "You're a damned good writer, hon."

What touched her even more was that he asked her about it from time to time. He didn't forget it. And once, he even mentioned a particular scene that had touched him. It had stuck with him.

He'd always supported her writing…at least emotionally supported it. Should she do the same with his?

If I can pursue my art, why can't he pursue his? She'd reduced their argument to this one question.

Tears stung her eyes. She blinked them away.

Because it's not art, Jim. It's dilettantism. It's ego. It's…nothing. It's…an odd sort of envy run amok.

The angry responses played like a tape loop: *look, you've told me a hundred times if you've told me once that you don't think what you do is art, writing those bodice rippers. They're not bodice-rippers, Jim! That's demeaning. I don't write that kind of romance. Whatever. The point is that I'm expressing myself, and it might pay off….*

She wished she could turn it off, but it was always there.

They'd married right out of college, both of them naïve and hopeful. Both had been the first generation in their families to go to college—her dad, who'd died when she was thirteen, had been a supervisor of the night shift at Bethlehem Steel, her mother a part-time receptionist at a doctor's office; Jim's father was a policeman, his one brother a Marine, and his mother a nurse. Both their dads had been in the service.

Their parents were baby boomers, but not the kinds who'd worn beads and protested. The kinds who'd gone to the Vietnam War and come back, angry, sobered, but not professional cynics. The kinds who were too busy staying one step above lower working class to take time for much else. So, Jim and Kate had both been left out of the whole Sixties nostalgia. In their households, it had merely been the usual longing for one's youth, not a movement.

After two years at a community college, she and Jim had gone to a local state college that had little name recognition, and they'd chosen majors based on their interests at the time. She'd chosen history, and he'd selected political science.

They'd had no idea what careers they could carve out with those degrees. They'd not realized that graduate studies, which neither was interested in, would have been required for any kind of meaningful work in their fields. They'd assumed — as had their families — that college got you better jobs and more money. Maybe it did for the well-connected. But for people like Kate and Jim, a college degree just meant they got in the door faster...for the same jobs they'd have had without the diplomas.

The first year they were married, she worked as a legal secretary, he as a teller at a bank. They'd had hopes of moving up or...something. They'd rented an apartment not far from their college — a garden apartment with trees outside the windows and good parking. They'd seen her mother or his family on weekends, and sometimes they'd driven out to the country to visit her sister, Becky, ten years older and raising two bright girls with her husband, Bob. Becky and Bob ran a small insurance agency together, but their true love was their farmette, into which they poured time and tenderness.

The Litany of Events, as Kate had started calling it, began a few days after their first anniversary. First, the good news. Kate, who'd beavered away silently and secretly on her writing, sold her first romance novel. Champagne corks popped, happiness reached its apex.

But then Jim lost his job when his branch closed, and he had trouble finding another one, mostly because he didn't seem to know what he wanted to do. While she worked on revisions to that first novel, afraid she'd not manage the small changes her editor wanted, afraid she'd get a call saying there'd been some mistake and her book wasn't really going to be published, Jim had finally lit on what he wanted to do. Not just banking. But investment banking. His father had a connection who knew somebody who knew somebody in New York, and Jim headed there one weekend for an informational interview, to find out the lay of the land and what was required. They even started talking of moving to New York, center of the publishing world, the literary world. Kate felt on her way, optimistic, happy that Jim, too, was feeling a sense of direction at last.

That was...before...

She shook her head. She had to get back to work — writing, looking for an agent. She would sell something besides the "bodice rippers." She blushed, thinking how she'd chided Jim for using that expression when she thought of them that way even if she didn't use the term.

She'd only started writing romance because she hadn't felt worthy of trying to join the lih-trah-chure crowd.

She heard the doorbell ring — the pizza was here — and Jim's voice, amiably talking to the deliveryman. But she wasn't ready to break bread with him yet. The closed door would signal she wasn't to be disturbed.

After her agent emails were sent, she pulled out Beatrice Rutherford's papers and started reading again, letting the story comfort her, excite her. More and more, she saw Beatrice's story as a ticket to the destination she wanted to reach in the publishing business and somehow, too, as the ticket back to where she and Jim had begun, deeply in love, intuitively supportive of each other, even in imperfect ways.

CHAPTER FIVE

THE MARCH OF TIME by Beatrice Rutherford
In New York, I learned several painful truths. I am not and never will be comfortable with a certain class of people. I wished all my life I could be at ease with those of great wealth or sophistication. After all, I believed with all my heart that God's children are the same in His eyes, no matter the circumstances of their birth. (And, yes, I came to realize this included those of a certain skin color, as well, so don't be judging me as a hypocrite on that score.) At the time of my move to New York, being a lady of the south, I also believed my lineage entitled me to some deference and respect. That disappeared when I landed in the big northern city. I was always on edge, a foreigner afraid of breaking the unspoken, unwritten rules of etiquette of a very civilized society.

And I was not, despite Mr. Flockstone's grand pronouncements, destined to be a singer of great repute. Madame Solinsky put the lie to that claim as soon as she heard me. She declared my voice "sweet" and even "charming," but not big enough to thrill the audiences of the major opera houses. Oh, I would do for a "comprimario" role here and there and would be a good addition to the Met's chorus. And, if I had the artistry — she seemed open to convincing but not settled on this matter—I might even do some recital work. As for making anything approaching a living from my voice? She seemed skeptical.

It didn't break my heart. I must admit to a certain relief, in fact. I'd never been comfortable on display, and when you're on stage, standing in the crook of that piano, hands clasped together…well, it's a hard thing to forget that you're asking folks to look at you, look at you. It's not that I don't enjoy attention. It's just that I like folks to find me, rather than me throwing myself at them.

I began to see myself in a clear mirror, realizing what I was and what I wasn't. *Began* to see—it took a long time for that process, a whole lifetime, in fact. But it started there in New York surrounded by folk who weren't like me. Being there around all that sophistication made me look afresh at what I considered pretty, and ruffles and bows lost their luster. I was a hick, I realized, and some people don't like hicks, even when we manage to educate ourselves in the finer things. I did sing opera, did I not? It didn't matter to a certain crowd. No matter how hard I tried, I'd not be their kind.

"Their kind" was running amok. Drinking everywhere, doing wild things, acting as if the world was ending right at the end of the week so they had to cram a lot of living in before turning the corner to Sunday. Was it living? Now when I look back on those years, I do wonder if we wasted a lot of time in our efforts to live each day to the fullest. Do you do that by reckless activity? Or are better memories built on slow, quiet thoughtfulness? Seems I remember those more than the laughing cut-up moments. I cringe when I remember some of the activities I joined in just to show I was part of that set.

On the other side, I saw and read a fair amount of scolding going on that irritated me with its puritanical selfishness; so I, like the rest of my generation, wasn't inclined to listen too much to the lectures, especially from those who'd cheered the march to ruinous war. I could do a fair amount of my own head shaking and scolding, but I was not inclined to abide it in others.

I do remember some serious young folks who seemed disappointed by their peers, which included me at the time, and I sometimes feel as though we wronged those men and women. We let them down. They were the ones who dragged us all through to the other side when things got bad later. They were the little red hens.

But back then, I was eager to let go of the old, whether it was good or not. I wasn't immune to wanting some of the fun, thinking the prim and proper set had ruined life for people like me, who'd seen their loves go off to battle and not come back. I started thinking about that too much, truth be told. So I tried as best I could to pack away my feelings of inferiority along with my ruffles and bows, to shed the worst of my Baptist strictures, and I straightened my shoulders and went about placing one foot in front of the other to join the party, as if this were a task I'd set my mind to.

I arranged a lesson now and then with Madame, just to make sure I wasn't wasting a God-given talent, and I looked for a job. I found one at an advertising agency, typing up invoices and doing some accounting.

A couple of young ladies in our department would get together every week on Friday nights. Imagine my surprise to discover this was no quilting group or sewing bee. They drank, in their apartments or at speakeasies.

Some form of gin, sometimes a whiskey. They danced to records and real jazz bands of sweating Negroes. They broke one rule after another, and I was confronted with the wherefore of such rules, often coming up blank with answers as to why I shouldn't give something a try. I began to think it had been a failure of my parents' generation not to have grounded us more in the why of things, just expecting us to soldier on as they had and to know. How judgmental we are in youth, doling out critiques to puritan and prodigal alike. So I broke the rules, happily. I smoked, I drank, I danced, I laughed and cursed. I flirted, too, but was careful with that when I heard someone whisper about me being a "tease."

I sometimes wished I could write a letter home to my momma, telling her how exciting my life was. But I couldn't share all that, of course. She would have been scandalized, for sure, and I wasn't cruel enough to flaunt my indiscretions in front of her. I knew some who did that sort of thing. It disturbed me to no end.

I broke every rule I ever knew except the big ones. And, as I found out later, I might have broken one of those, too, if my stubborn self-regard didn't save me at the hour of temptation.

So, for many months, I toiled away during the day, happy to be busy, and strolled or read at night in a little rooming house filled with other women like me. Their radios blared at night when I came home, their personal garments dried on racks in the bathroom, their inexpensive perfumes floated down the hallway.

On weekends, I got together with my friends from the agency, and it felt sometimes as if we were working on the solution to a problem, talking and laughing to all hours, smoke curling in to the night air, whiskey-filled glasses sparkling in the light, all with a certain drive and passion. We never did solve that problem. Never figured out even what it was.

At the agency, I worked on one floor, *he* on another. But as soon as I saw him, leaving one day for lunch with some of his buddies, his eyes caught mine, and I was done for.

It was as if Jeremy had stared me in the face. Those bright eyes, that "Irish" look to him that took the world too seriously and not seriously enough all at once, that made you feel like you shared some secret with him even though you didn't even know him.

After Jeremy, I felt as if that world he'd introduced me to, the world of a man loving a woman and woman a man, was a shrine of some kind. And I was appropriately reverential when approaching it. It was a trembling kind of approach, it was such a sacred thing, you see. So I avoided it the same way I ended up avoiding church itself during those wild days after the War. Too rich for my blood, it was as if I was thinking. Too high for a girl like me. I'd found it once and wouldn't again.

Love isn't like that, though, something apart from the everyday living we do. Yes, I think it's a sacred thing, and it requires, as I was soon to find out, sacrifices of Biblical proportions at times. But those come in the midst of day after day of endurance, sometimes so much endurances it makes you wonder why you thought it was special in the first place.

At the start of my journey with them, though, I was of a mind to let the dust grow on my own icon of Love. Jeremy. I didn't want to touch that memory with something new.

I didn't think about spending the rest of my life alone, but that's how it came to pass, mostly because the one shrine I would approach was the temple of Scott and Zelda. My affection for him acted as a wall protecting me from other entanglements. I let that happen, I admit. But maybe part of me never was willing to give up on loving Jeremy. It was a way of keeping him alive still, and keeping me of a mind what we had was unique. That *I* was unique.

I wasn't different from many a girl at that time. War widows abounded. Women past the first bloom of youth were hard-pressed to find a good man. We were our own army of single old maids. Married once, breathless at the thought of it, too afraid to try again. We fashioned love something apart with our grief.

I'd learned that a lot of life was just putting one foot in front of the other to get through. I sometimes grew impatient with those who didn't want to walk. I grew impatient with Them many a time. But this was after they became real to me, not some dream. And when I met him, he was a dream.

I asked about him in the bookkeeping department. That's Scott, they told me. He fancies himself a writer. They laughed about it in our group. They didn't take him seriously, thought he put on airs and was too big for his own britches. I wrote Momma about him:

"…there's a young man here, so earnest and true that I think you'd like him. He gave me a flower yesterday, one he'd purloined from a cart on the street. Oh, don't be thinking he really stole it. It had broken off a bouquet, and it would have gone to waste. It's the brightest daisy, still blooming in my little apartment even as I write this."

There is a moment in that *Gatsby* of his, that wonderful story that just can't be told but his way, a story you want to keep reading and you want to keep hearing him tell to you, well, there's a moment where his Daisy, his Zelda, tells Nick she's been everywhere and seen everything. "Sophisticated—God, I'm sophisticated!" she tells him.

But it's a sham, a bit of fakery, to cover her real heartbreak at finding out the world—the everywhere and everything—didn't care about her as much as she thought it did, as much as she might have cared about it. You see, Daisy's something of a cipher, isn't she? Did she love Jay or Tom or just herself? I like to think she loved Jay truest of all, but it broke her spirit when she couldn't have him, so she decided that's what being sophisticated meant, giving up tenderness and kindness and honesty for the accumulation of comforts and consolations.

I became partial to her character more as years went by, as I eventually became warmer to her model, Zelda. I think I began to see in her more of ...him. He with his sad eyes and desire to please, to be loved. He had this honesty about him, this freshness. You knew that deep down there was a kind and tender soul, but he covered it more and more over the years. With that sophistication Daisy winks about, as if to say she never wanted to be that way, but the world required it.

He was a real charmer, he was, and if I was as wise as I fancied myself back then, I would have realized he wasn't for me. I knew his heart was set on another. That was a topic of conversation in our little cabal, as well, something the girls would gobble about on our Friday evenings, listening to records of smooth-voiced men singing about their gals. He has a girl, they all said, and I thought she would be some cold fish, a New York sophisticate not really good enough for him. But when I heard she was a Southern belle, well, the wind went out of me for sure. I couldn't compete with one of my own, especially one who apparently held such magical powers. For he did talk to me about her, you see. He and I ended up at a lunch counter, and he'd received a letter from her that had set him in a stew. She was apparently gadding about Montgomery with this old beau or that new friend, and it tore him up inside.

I tried comforting him, offering the usual about true love will out and all that. What I was really thinking: she doesn't deserve you. You deserve a woman who will stand by you and tell you you're the most brilliant writer alive. I was willing to apply for the job, but he didn't seem to think of that position as open.

You see, I was in love with him as a writer by then because I'd offered to retype some of his work for him. Once I heard of his aspirations, I ignored all the clucking of our coop and told him I'd heard he wrote, that I was an admirer of those who strove, and that I'd be happy to help him since I could type.

I typed a draft of *This Side of Paradise* for him. Typed it several times, in fact, sometimes mourning the words lost in his changes. I fell in love with the romanticism of him. I knew what he was talking about in that book, falling hard for someone and having it yanked away. Oh, my, but my heart did break afresh, even though his book was as far from Jeremy and me as we were from the south up there in Manhattan. But what he wrote about was bigger than the people in his story, that feeling of drifting and yearning and wanting it all to be bigger than it was, to be ... remembered. To be imprinted on your time. And wanting that first love to be the only one. The Love. With a capital "L."

I think that idea is the one that saved me from him. I would have given in to the pull for more earthly longings to be satisfied if not for that notion. There had been but one man for me, Jeremy. And Scott seemed to know that, even though he didn't know a thing about my dead husband, not his name, not that he'd existed at all.

As I watched him struggle, grinding away at jingles about tooth powder and hair grease, I ached for him, knowing he must have felt his artistry just oozing away being wasted on some prosaic things. And I ached for his unrequited love because I knew Zelda couldn't love him if she wasn't rushing up to be with him, to encourage him, to cheer for him.

So, in an odd way, his success with *Paradise* — when it sold, making it possible for Zelda to marry him — was a mixed joy for me. I wanted to be happy for him. Instead, I found myself jealous of sharing him with the world, and especially with her.

Before he had that first success, he was striving so hard to be a man of his times. That was part of his charm, how hard he tried. He might only be able to afford a baloney sandwich, but he wore a suit from Blake & Swithe and specially tailored shirts, cuff links of ebony and pearl, and his hair was always perfectly groomed. A barber spent some time on that head, that's for sure.

At a lunch counter one day, he sheepishly searched his pockets for change for a tip, and I told him not to bother, I'd handle it. He'd grinned from ear to ear, thanking me with mock chivalry and a string of words coated in sweet caramel. And then he'd added, "You're a peach, Bea, a real Georgia peach, and I know a thing or two about the flora of the south and its enticing appeal. I can now get my weekly shave at Grauber's!"

It didn't surprise or offend me that he'd saved himself from tipping because he had a more luxurious use of his money in mind. That, too, was part of his appeal—his honesty about his nature, as if he expected the world to love him as he was. What bothered me more was that he didn't remember I wasn't from Georgia.

Later, his honest approach to the world was ground out of him somewhat, letting a less flattering wariness that sometimes oozed into arrogance color his attitude. But if he was ground down, it was life and its troubles that did it, and the whole publishing business, too, with its peacocks strutting around trying to be better and worthier than the rest by making him feel low. I noticed that in the music world, as well—how so many must burnish their talent by cruelly pointing out the dullness of others, whether true or not. There's no need for that.

And, yes, Zelda, too, did a fair share of wearing out the sweet spots of his nature. For many years, I resented her something awful for doing that, laying at her feet all the reasons why he changed from charming naïf to jaded egoist.

The very honesty and forthrightness I admired in him, I disdained in her. Why, she went swimming while carrying little Scottie. She, as big as, well, obscenely big, when women were discreet about such things, was asked to leave the pool. That was in Montgomery, and I only heard about the incident later, when they came back to New York after the birth. And I remember thinking: What did she expect? We were civilized, not African savages baring our flesh to the sun. How scandalous! And how thoughtless to give Scott such trouble.

Now, however, I have a different view of such things, brought on by the passage of time and my increasing knowledge of her. She'd meant no harm, hadn't intended to flaunt her pregnancy in anyone's face.

She was just…who she was. And she expected the world to love her that way because she loved the world in her own fashion. Just as he was who he was in that blessed time before fame and responsibility crushed in on him.

They ended up having that little babe in his home of St. Paul, and that's when he cribbed a note for Gatsby's Daisy, straight from Zelda's mouth: *I hope it's beautiful and a fool. A beautiful little fool.*

Even that kind of stealing from her I didn't mind in those years. He was the great artist in my mind, creating something sweet and ageless. And I was just lucky to be around as the words flowed into eternity.

CHAPTER SIX

HE WAITED FOR HER. He resisted the aroma of pepperoni, melted cheese, greasy crust, and he waited until she was done working, until the pizza was cold, so they could eat together.

Over their late dinner of cold pizza and beer in the kitchen, Jim asked her about her writing. She'd told him her stories before, reading long passages, even complete novels to him in the evenings, and he'd sometimes made suggestions for a plot twist—what if this happened, he'd say. And sometimes they were good ideas. Now she didn't talk about writing. She talked about the business of writing, filling him in on the latest from Alice and her fears that she'd be dropped, on what her writer friends were saying in emails, how the erotica genre was selling like hotcakes, how vampires were still in, how tattooed male torsos decorated virtually every cover, how more and more writers were forgoing traditional publishing and striking out on their own into digital self-publishing.

Should she go that route? She'd read the blog post by John Jackson deriding self-published authors, how they only went that way because they'd failed elsewhere. If she chose that path, it would certainly be because of some failure, her failure to sell the stories that she wanted to write. His barbs, while cruel, resonated with her, dulled her sense of accomplishment.

Bea Rutherford was right that artists often dragged each other down as they tried to clamber to the top. But that didn't take the sting out of negative remarks, especially when they might hold a milligram of poisonous truth.

"Oh, babe," Jim said, putting his hand over hers. "Don't let Alice get to you. You know you're good. Look at all the fan mail you get."

But even that had dwindled over the past year, which just seemed to confirm Alice's assessment. She needed to change to find new readers. But the new readers she really wanted weren't romance ones.

"I need to find a new agent, I think," she said softly.

He ran his fingers through his thick hair and grimaced. He knew how little she liked that job.

"You're published. Can't you submit to editors on your own?"

She sighed. "Yeah. I guess. Probably." She took her plate to the sink. They might eat pizza, but damned if they'd use paper plates. She had some standards.

"It takes so much time, though. Researching who's buying what. Querying. Wondering if you targeted the right one. In theory," she said, her voice dripping with skepticism, "the agent is supposed to have nurtured relationships with editors and know their tastes."

"In theory." He cleared his own place and took his things to the sink where he proceeded to load the dishwasher. Kate leaned against the counter to his side and felt his warmth radiate toward her, giving her comfort.

"All agents sound wonderful at first. They all tell you you can contact them any time. They give you a big spiel about what they'll do for you."

"Well, I guess they're not going to say anything but that," he said, not looking at her. "I mean, they're not going to tell you how many books they don't sell."

"Maybe that's a good question to ask—what's your selling percentage? Of the books you submit, how many sell?"

"Do you think they even keep that data?"

She shrugged. Even if they did, would they share an accurate version of it?

"Do you have any preferences?" he asked.

"A couple. Some agents who are selling stuff like mine." Like her coming-of-age story, not romance. "But the problem is, I'm moving in a new direction, so it's like I'm unpublished. In that area." Jim knew about her aspirations.

"Is that wise?" he said now, rubbing his head. "I mean, if it looks like the cash cow is romance, maybe you should get an agent who does that, too?"

"It's hard to find one who does both! And even if I did, chances are they'd take me on for the romance and not work hard on my other stuff. I've had that experience already! I'm the cash cow. My romance writing." She glared at him. That was the problem—she was the cash cow. Even here. He needed to enter the cash cow barn.

"You know what would help?" she said after a few moments. "If we didn't need to depend on the romance writing. If I could just write what I wanted...." Translation: *Why don't you stop dicking around with that painting stuff and get a job, Jim?*

Now he leaned against the kitchen island. "I'm working on that, babe."

She couldn't help herself. She let out an audible sigh. He was referring to his painting being the solution.

"We need something soon if my next contract doesn't come through," she said through gritted teeth.

"Come here. Let me show you." She thought at first he meant he'd show her how much he loved her, and she wanted that embrace, despite her irritation with him. So she was disappointed when he headed for the basement, expecting her to follow.

"It's not the same thing at all!" She stood with her hands on her hips, staring at Jim's creation, a spattered piece of canvas on the basement floor. Her head ached. She shouldn't have had the beer. Her headache was made worse by the odor of fresh paint creeping into the rest of the house.

When she'd followed him downstairs, he'd proudly displayed his latest, telling her he intended to try to sell it to a downtown gallery. This was a first. Up until this moment, his "hobby" had remained, as most hobbies, something he did for his own personal pleasure — and her torment, she often thought. But to have him trying to peddle this as "art"? It gagged her.

"Why not? You're always telling me what you do isn't art but it's what keeps a roof over our heads. You keep trying to get those artsy fartsies to pay attention to you, and they won't give you the time of day even though what you do actually sells. You know, people actually read it."

She rubbed her temples as he daubed another bit of blue on to the canvas, smearing what little pattern he'd created. Her gaze traveled to the can he was using – "Sky Blue Fantasy" left over from painting their bedroom. He'd tried, it seemed to her, to do a pattern of peacock "eyes." Or maybe it was waves? Or…something. They were symmetrical – that showed skill, at least.

"I might not produce art. But I use skill!" Her hands fisted at her sides. "This – this isn't even skill. This is…bullshit. Pure bullshit!"

To her surprise, he didn't fight her assessment. He stood back and rubbed his forehead with his knuckle, squinting at his great artistic effort, leaving a blue smudge above his right eye. Slowly, he nodded his head.

"Maybe." Then he turned and grinned. "Which is precisely why it will sell."

"Get a job!" she said at last. She'd never articulated it, only hoped he'd see her distress, her desperation, and do the right thing.

"What?"

"Stop this lunacy and just get a job, Jim. Please!" Despite her best efforts, she started to cry.

He looked confused, as if he was genuinely surprised at the request.

"I – I am trying to. I mean, I thought selling this would…"

This…this…masterpiece…wasn't what she'd envisioned.

She ran up the stairs into the kitchen, bawling when she banged her foot against the refrigerator corner, slamming cupboard doors looking for fresh grounds and a filter to make some coffee. She was so angry that her hand shook, and she cracked the carafe in the sink when she turned on the faucet.

By the time Jim came up to comfort her, she was sitting cross-legged on the floor, the detached plastic handle to the carafe in her hands, coffee grounds spilled on the counter.

"Oh, Kate," Jim said, sitting across from her and taking the handle from her. "You poor thing."

She leaned into him, hating herself for being so easily mollified by his strong hug, his tender kisses on her forehead, wishing she could remain steely and aloof.

When she'd cried herself out, she looked at him and asked hoarsely: "What are you going to do?"

His face looked so eager, reminding her of how he'd looked boarding that train to New York years ago. "I'll make it work. And you…you get an agent. A good one. If Alice buys your next book, make her pay for it. Really pay."

She let him hug her again, and soon their embraces led to a different kind of comfort.

෴

For two days, it snowed, wiping spring anticipation away. If the mid-Atlantic region teased, this state tortured. She watched as an icy mess glazed their driveway, temperatures staying below freezing. Meanwhile, the sky hung like a ledge of gray cloud over them, the gray ledge that seemed to arrive every fall from the northwest and linger, sometimes tripping away for a visit to an unlucky friend, perhaps, but always finding its way home. This, too, she disliked. She'd come to realize—discovering, as many people did, what she loved after she'd lost it—that she drew comfort, inspiration, and joy from skyscapes. Here, the mountains and the clouds conspired to keep those views cramped and rare.

She disciplined herself not to ask Jim what he was doing about getting work. She needed to trust him, she told herself. She needed to believe that he loved her enough to do this one thing for her. She heard him on the phone a few times. And she noticed his "art" was missing from the basement. Part of her knew that he probably hadn't destroyed it, that he had gone through with his mission to sell it to a gallery. She cringed at that possibility, sometimes feeling embarrassed when she went into town, passing the two galleries there. Were they laughing behind their closed doors and shaded windows at them? Everyone knew everyone in a small town.

While she pushed those thoughts aside, she worked hard on her own goals. She took more earnest steps to land an agent and was pleased when a few responded to her queries about one of her manuscripts.

Oh, not one of her romance ones. She didn't hide the fact that she wrote romance, but she was pitching her coming-of-age story, one that she had worked on since she'd first started writing, a Serious Story that had stayed in the back of her mind refusing to let go, that she'd written in spare moments when inspiration struck or the aftereffects of a glass of wine unlocked her true muse. This story was the one that had called to her even as she'd penned the other non-romance material, the manuscripts for which she'd now had "book funerals," putting them away in desk drawers, in computer files, after agents failed to sell them.

But while she waited for those agents to read her masterpiece, she still had to finish the romance she'd promised Alice. Alice was enthusiastic after Kate had sent early pages.

Wonderful — just the right note! But...maybe have them have sex on the train after all? What a way to start a story!

She'd smiled to herself. No sex scene yet. She briefly thought – hoped – she could keep deferring it, with Alice getting so caught up in the tale that she'd see Kate's point. You didn't need fifty shades of sex to sell folks on reading....

She'd made progress on the story, having hero and heroine reunite after their near-one-night stand five years earlier. Now the heroine had moved to the East Coast and ended up doing business with hero. She was working for a New Jersey mayor with higher political aspirations — Alice had resisted that a bit, fearing romance readers wouldn't want politics in the mix, but Kate had assured her it would be "apolitical" politics, with no policy discussions to speak of, just good human drama. Drama and sparks. Sparks and "heat," and "sizzle," and lust, lust, lust, with a capital L! She realized she was having too much fun making Alice happy, loving to get her "I'm fanning myself, I'm in love with these two, Bravo!" emails whenever Kate fed her new material.

Hero was now about forty, heroine in her late twenties. Hero regretted never following up with heroine except through some occasional emails and holiday cards. Ditto heroine. Both had had relationships in the interim, with heroine even getting engaged at one point. That had caused hero a dark moment, and he'd scaled back on contact until it had dribbled to nothing...but he'd never forgotten her, had never forgotten her laugh, her smile, her green eyes. More than once, he'd awakened from a dream trembling with desire for her, her eyes seeming to appear in the distance, over a moonlit sea, winking at him to find her.

Now heroine was at hero's house after having imbibed too much the night before during a business dinner and engaged in many provocative acts on the way to his house, provocative acts Alice had loved—*oh, that's good, Kate,* she'd written, *I love how you have her arousing him even when he's driving.* He resisted her, not wanting to take advantage of her when she was under the influence—he was a hero, was he not? It took all his self-control to peel himself from her warm, enticing body, but he eventually got her to bed—to sleep. He almost gave in when she seductively kissed him and pulled him toward her, but he wouldn't do something he was afraid she'd regret in the morning. Besides, a phone call interrupted their advances. Nonetheless, he was…a hero! So he left her sleeping and retreated to his study. And there, over a glass of aged whiskey, he realizes he is in love with this charming vixen, had fallen for her five years ago the moment he'd met her and felt the electric connection. But he'd devoted his life to raising his younger brother, see, after their parents had perished in an accident, and he'd not dated seriously in a long time. But now that he's met Belinda, he wants more than a one-night stand. Or an almost-one-night stand. He wants to move the focus to something beyond the physical…he wants his one true love.

CHAPTER SEVEN

WISHFUL THINKING – CHAPTER TWO

Five years of occasional emails, cards – a particularly sweet and loving one when his dog had died – even a boozy New Year's Eve call that had delighted him at first, saddened him later. She only thought of him when tipsy? In that way?

He'd thought of her more often than he liked admitting. In fact, seeing her again had made him realize just how much she'd populated his thoughts. Every day for the past five years something related to her had floated through his mind, even if it was an ephemeral impression, like an audio imprint, or a sand indentation, quickly smoothed out by the next onslaught of reality, work, life. Gone when he sought it out again with clear head.

When he'd seen her come into his office – my God, he'd felt like a schoolboy. Damp palms, stammering introductions, a lump in his throat, that damned tightening.

The nature of their coupling – or almost coupling – the tantalizing moment of "could have been" – surely that was responsible for this connection, this yearning. This Lust.

He wasn't interested in mere lust. With dismay, he realized he'd have to ask her out on a real date. It made him gag to think of it. So pedestrian. He wanted it to remain magic. But even so, they couldn't keep teasing each other. They owed it to each other to see what was what. Or at least, he owed it to her. Gentlemanly thing to do and all that rot.

Saturday night. The double date with his brother, Chris, and his girlfriend, Sarah Chang. That sounded good. A double date presented less temptation. They'd have to talk to each other, get to know each other. Instead of just groping each other. Maybe he'd find she was an empty-headed kook. And she'd discover he was a boring reactionary. And they'd part, grateful not to have become entangled, glad to have had their fantasies crumbled because, damn it, better to be realistic and disappointed than hopeful and disappointed. That always hurt more.

Fantasies, while they lasted, were exquisite, though. His body heated just thinking about how she'd touched him in the car, the things she'd purred, the promises to do more, and then he'd thought of nothing but those word pictures, about her, naked on the bed, unashamed, wanton…beckoning, open, wet, hot…. Him strong, over her, ready…

That had taken willpower he hadn't realized he had to step back, to say no, to smile and wish her good-night. No, not willpower, he realized. Care. Great care. And his damned need to know what was what. And that saving call from Chris.

He gulped his drink. It was still early. Too early to go to bed. The strange yellow light of a rainy gloaming was past, darkness tinged with wet-concrete odors, the scent of promise.

He didn't want to risk waking Belinda, so he wasn't about to watch television. He walked out of the kitchen back into the study, a small room with a desk diagonally across the far corner, an old leather chair behind it, and bookshelves everywhere. He went over to one and started perusing the volumes. Something long, he thought. Dreary.

His eye caught sight of a row of recent best sellers, things he'd picked up based on this literary critic's raves or that literature journal review. After picking one up, he remembered why he'd abandoned it—two-hundred pages of poetic description and no story that had felt three times as long by the moment he'd finished it. He tried another. Oh, yes, he'd dropped this one because it was nothing more than mawkish sorrow masquerading as depth—all Eros and no Psyche, just grief designed to titillate in its own way. He looked at still another, but it was one he'd already read, a romantic novel by a man named Claus Flames. Hmm...it had made him think there was something of depth to romance novels, and he remembered how it had been reviewed and featured in the *Times* and elsewhere. Surely other people wrote romance, too... who were they? He found a mystery, acclaimed by genre and literary Brahmins, and settled in. At least the mystery would propel him through.

Still, he found himself staring into space at the end of each page, not even able to recount what he had just read there. He relived the moments in the car on the way home when Belinda had been driving him mad, leaning over, playing with him, laughing, teasing.... He relived their kiss. And he started to worry.

He was forty now and felt even older. When he had seen her again earlier that day, he had realized with stunning clarity that the chances of finding another

Belinda Remington, of making that kind of lightning connection, were extremely remote. And he wasn't really interested in prowling the singles-scene looking for it anyway. He wanted it to bump into him on a train.

Belinda, on the other hand, was almost ten years younger than he was. She might want nothing more than a hot and furious fling. She might not want to settle down. She'd been engaged, after all, and ended it.

You're as bad as your clients, Jake, he said to himself, thinking back to the warm glow the memories of the evening inspired in him. Looking for signs to bolster what you want to have happen, rather than seeing reality for what it is. You're engaging in wishful thinking.

❧

Bold morning light streamed through the window. He still smelled the aftereffects of the rain, the damp, erotic scent of earth and greenery, as he searched his cabinets and refrigerator for something to offer her for breakfast. After raising his brother for so many years, he was a damn fine cook. An omelet, he thought, with fresh fruit, whole wheat toast, and some turkey sausage on the side. He set to fixing it.

She straggled into the room, looking bleary-eyed and hurting.

"Is that coffee?" she asked weakly, eyeing his machine. She had the afghan wrapped around her. Her brows creased with pain. Seeing a nearby chair, she collapsed into it, holding her head between her hands as she leaned in to the table.

"Any preferences?" He held up the K-cup tray.

"Anything with caffeine," she murmured.

He popped in a packet of Columbian, and within seconds placed a steaming mug in front of her. "Cream, sugar?" he asked, but she shook her head ever so slightly before slowly sipping the brew, bending head to cup rather than trusting her hands.

He frowned with concern. "I'm fixing you something." He didn't like seeing her in pain, yet he struggled with how much to do. He didn't want to hover. After he'd described what he had in mind, she smiled.

"Oh, man, that's exactly what I'd like," she said. "How did you know?" She managed to hold the mug to her lips and swallow some more coffee.

"Good guess," he said. He whipped the eggs to a froth, put a pan on low heat, started the sausage. After he popped some bread into the toaster, he made his own cup of java.

"Not tea?" she managed to ask, and he would have smiled except it struck him that there was something wrong with not knowing he preferred coffee to tea when she'd been so eager to know him in other intimate ways.

"Lost that preference, if I ever had it, a long time ago," he said.

"What time is it?" she asked.

"Just about seven," he said.

"I have to get back," she muttered. "Is there a morning train? There has to be a morning train. A commuter thing." Her new job was in New Jersey, he remembered. Working for a mayor there. A mayor wanting polling services. She quickly took another gulp of coffee, clearly struggling with nausea.

"You don't do this often, I hope," he said before thinking of how rude it sounded. And how old. As if he was a reprimanding schoolmaster.

"No!" She looked wounded, and that soothed him, that she was offended at the suggestion. He'd like a little time to explore their relationship before offending her.

He had the breakfast ready in no time. The toast popped out, and Jake placed the two slices on a plate next to the perfectly cooked eggs. He set them before her with a fork, knife and some butter and a jar of jam. When she made no move to retrieve them, he buttered the toast for her.

"Do you want some jelly?" he asked. "I have strawberry."

"Strawberry's my favorite," she said.

"Mine, too," he said, smearing some on the toast for her. He watched, gratified, when she tucked in, hungrily devouring the meal.

"You must think I'm pretty silly," she said after awhile. She had consumed every last bit of the omelet and sausage, most of the fruit and drunk all the coffee. He stood to get her another cup.

"I don't," he said, placing some bread in the toaster for himself. And then softly, as if surprising himself with his honesty: "I think you're wonderful." As he sat across from her again, he noticed her blush. The afghan dropped away off her shoulders, revealing the white dress. Then he remembered her underwear upstairs on the chair.

He cleared his throat. "There's something you should know about last night," he began.

Blushing more deeply, her eyes squinted together, obviously waiting for the bad news. She must have remembered the car ride and the kiss, Jake thought, watching her.

"Nothing happened." He put his hands around his coffee mug, hugging the warm cup in an effort to keep himself from reaching out for her.

She brightened considerably. "You're a gentleman!" She sounded surprised.

"I wish I could lay full claim to that label," he said slowly. "Let's just say that we were interrupted by a phone call at a *very* strategic moment."

She smiled again, wider, carefree. "We seem to have a habit of starting things and not finishing them."

"Maybe it's fate," he said. "Maybe something's telling us we should go a little more slowly."

"I don't normally..." She stopped herself, laughing. Then, she reached up to grab her obviously aching head. "...do that sort of thing. Go so fast, that is. My pace is usually more like that of a languid turtle."

"Languid turtle sounds fine by me. I'm generally considered the King of Inertia by my colleagues. Maintain the status quo," he said, chuckling as well. "Say, do you want an ice bag for your head?"

"I think I'll be okay. It only hurts when I laugh now."

"Do you need to call someone?"

"I should call my office. When they open. I should really try to get back, too. The mayor has a charity event this morning. I was going to go with him."

"Is it crucial you be there?"

"It's a standard 'grip-and-grin' type of thing where he presents some check to a local community club that raised a bunch of matching funds for a city grant. Usually, I go to these things. Sometimes not."

"Maybe this is a perfect 'not' time," he said, devising a plan. Today was Friday. Tomorrow was Saturday. Date day. Hadn't she said she had a sister in Maryland?

"Your sister," he said, changing subjects. "Do you visit her often?"

"About once a month," she answered, nonplussed by his shift in topics.

"Maybe you should just hang around and go there this weekend." That blasted sense of hopefulness started building in him, a real feeling of pressure pushing on his chest. His palms were as sweaty as a teenager's.

"I *was* planning on coming down this weekend to visit her," she said. "But I don't have any clothes with me. And...my office will wonder. Everybody'll wonder. What the hell am I doing in Baltimore this morning in a strange man's house? I really should get back."

He grimaced. A strange man's house? "And turn right around and come back to Maryland to see your sister?" he said, starting to feel let down. "As for clothes, take my credit card. Buy a closet full." He'd buy her a car if that's what it took to keep her here.

She raised her eyebrows, clearly surprised at the offer. "Aren't you the Daddy Warbucks!"

Ouch. Not an image he liked.

"I meant...don't waste a trip back to New Jersey just because you don't have a set of clothes to change into."

She thought a few moments about his suggestion. "But a whole day, Jake. I could be working."

He loved hearing her say his name.

"All right. Work. Come into my office this afternoon. For a meeting. That's work."

He walked to the coffeemaker to get another cup for himself. With his back to her, trying to sound nonchalant, he continued.

"And since you're going to be in town anyway," he said, looking into the backyard and not at her, "I could take you out on a real date. My brother Chris and a friend of his are going out tomorrow night. We could join them."

He held his breath while he waited for her answer. It seemed to take hours before she finally responded, and he fought wars within that time. "That actually sounds nice," she said slowly. "Very tempting."

Still not looking at her, he waited. He heard the "but" in that sentence.

"But I don't have a change of clothes," she repeated. "And I'm not letting you buy me some when we've just met."

But they'd not just met. They'd known each other forever, hadn't they? It seemed that way, on some deep unspoken level. In his mind, they'd made love. And if her performance last night was any indication, she'd held the same fantasies. Spectacular fantasies.

"If it bothers you, just pay me back." He turned and smiled.

She looked up at him and returned his smile. The radiance was beginning to come back into her face as the pain receded. "Okay. You've convinced me. I'll call my office and tell them I won't be in, and then hightail it out to my sister's. You don't need to schedule any phony meetings. I'll spend the time shopping with Rosemary instead."

Jake felt like lifting her up and....kissing her. And more. Much more. From the slow blush creeping up her cheeks, she might be having similar thoughts.

❧

After she had called her office, he offered to drive her to her sister's house, but she refused. "If Rosemary gets one look at you," she said, laughing, "she'll be badgering me mercilessly all weekend. I'll get a cab to the train station and hop on the MARC."

"But she'll have to see me tomorrow night anyway," he said, scooping up his car keys from the vestibule table where he had thrown them the night before. "I'll pick you up."

"Uh-uh," Belinda said. She was sitting on the stairs, the afghan pulled tight around her body, while she clasped the mug between her hands as if it were a lifeline. "I'll meet you at the restaurant. I can borrow Rosemary's car. That way, I'll be sure I won't imbibe too much again. And besides," she continued, "then I'll keep Rosemary from hovering over you and pressing you with all sorts of uncomfortable hints."

"Like what?" He stood by the door, not really wanting to leave. For a moment an image of a languorous morning amid tousled sheets swept through his mind.

"Oh, like what a terrific wife I would make. How she keeps telling me to settle down. And the questions – she would ask you a hundred of them, each one more focused and none of them subtle. 'Is there any mental illness in your family? Have you ever been convicted of a crime? Have you ever been married? Do you have any kids? Are you interested in children?'"

"Let me see – Not that I know of. No. No. No. And yes – in case she asks *you*," Jake said with a smile. He studied her face for a reaction but couldn't read anything beyond tired good nature. "Even if she doesn't meet me, won't she still be curious? Or are you planning on hiding our date from her? Telling a little white lie?"

"The thought did cross my mind," she said. Not what he wanted to hear. "But I don't like lying. I'll tell her. I'll tell her the truth. You're a business associate."

A business associate. Damn. Definitely not what he wanted to hear. A deep disappointment settled in, but he shook it off. He would woo her. Step by step. "Well, you know where the shower is. Just lock the door when you leave," he said, opening it. "And don't hesitate to call me if you need anything."

"Thanks. You've been really wonderful about this," she said, her lips turned up in happy cheer. "Oh, wait—" She got up. "My purse—where did I leave it?"

"You dropped it," he said, closing the door behind him. "It's in the living room. I'll go get it."

She nodded, and as he brushed by her, she caught his hand.

"Thanks. I'm such a bother." Her eyes searched his. Something inside him changed gears, something...tightened.

"No, you're not."

"I've probably already made you late." She seemed to be deliberately lingering, as if she wanted him to know something.

"I've been later," he said, wondering if he was misreading her, if he was so hungry for her that he'd assume she was being suggestive just by her touch.

Oh, to hell with it.

He placed his hand on her waist and crushed her to him and then against the wall, leaning in for a hard kiss that left no doubt as to what his suggestion would be, if she were open to it. He felt her respond, her hands kneading his back, her mouth hungrily opening to his, her hips pressing against him, and then the slightest release to let him know he could conquer her, take her. She let him push her fully against the wall, as if he had full control of her waiting body.

"I know you were good last night," she whispered when he pulled away. "But why not be naughty this morning?" She grabbed his hand. "I need a shower. Join me."

CHAPTER EIGHT

"AN AGENT LIKES me!" Kate practically shouted into the phone at her sister, Becky. "I'm thinking of going to New York to meet her. You have to go with me. Will you?"

"Why do you have to meet her?" Becky asked, tone skeptical. Outside of Jim, Becky was Kate's biggest cheerleader, but she had a practical streak that meant she didn't suffer fools gladly.

"She doesn't want to represent me...yet...I mean, she isn't keen on the manuscript I sent but on me as a writer, and I thought if I met her..."

She wasn't sure what she thought. She'd been thrilled to get the email from Ranier Thomason that morning, telling her what a terrific writer she was, how the manuscript Kate had sent didn't quite suit her, but she'd love to talk and see more from her. After a series of impersonal rejections, this had been an amazing uplifting moment, especially as it had come on the heels of a discouraging note from Alice saying she liked where "Jake and Belinda are headed, but you really need to get the physicality of the relationship moving faster. We're all adults here." If she heard that phrase one more time — *we're all adults here* — she was going to sit down on the floor, screaming, banging her fists and feet into the hardwood.

Not only had the timing been good, but Ranier was with a prestigious agency, one that represented literary novelists, not genre writers. If Ranier Thomason had taken her work seriously, that meant something. That meant...she was a real writer, worthy of respect.

"Well, I guess it always helps to see someone face-to-face."

"I'll pay for your ticket. We can meet at Penn Station," Kate urged. "Have lunch somewhere fancy. Gab."

"Well, you've tempted me. Sure, I'll go. Just for a day, right?"

"Thanks so much. I need the backup."

"No, you don't," Becky said flatly. "You're just scared because you think she's better than you. But she's not. You're just as good as anybody."

And that is precisely why I want you there with me, thought Kate.

After getting a few good dates from Becky that would work for her schedule, Kate turned to the computer and pulled up her email. With trembling fingers, she began her response:

Dear Ms. Thomason...

No, she'd signed her email "Ranier."

Dear Ranier,

I'm so happy to hear you liked my writing...

Did that sound too Sally Fieldish—you like me, you really like me....

I'm so pleased you like my writing. Would it be possible to talk...

No, "talk" could mean a phone call, and Kate wanted to meet her, to "seal the deal" on her representation as soon as Kate had an appropriate manuscript.

Would it be possible to meet? I'm going to be in New York on one of these dates....

She checked the dates Becky had given her and typed them in as possibilities.

If you're available on any of those days, I could stop by....

She finished the note with the usual pleasantries, signing it "Best, Kate," and hit Send.

Now she just needed to find something to do to keep her mind off waiting for a reply.

Restless, she Googled Ranier Thomason, looking for more information on her than she'd found at the agent query website and Publishers Marketplace.

With heart-stopping excitement, she discovered this agency had been *his* agency. F.Scott's agency!

She sat back in her chair as if pushed there. No, it couldn't be! This was Fate. Ranier Thomason was destined to be her agent. She couldn't wait to tell Becky, Jim.

Then, she thought of Beatrice Rutherford's papers. Surely Ranier would love to see them!

She went back to her email and composed a quick note about them, giving the history of the discovery, how she was typing them up in her spare time. Within seconds of sending her email, a response came in: "What an incredible find! Please, do bring them..." And then she agreed to one of the dates Kate had mentioned.

"Thank you, Beatrice," Kate whispered to the air. "You just landed me my agent."

She dropped notes to Jackie and Marie with the big news — all of it, including the F.Scott part.

Then she went off to find Jim. She should have told him before talking to Becky, but he would have squinted at her plan to ask her sister to go with her. He wouldn't have said anything; his look would have communicated his disapproval. And she needed Becky there. She needed her to hail taxis for her, to sit and scowl, to be a watchdog and witness should she forget any moment of this momentous possibility.

He was in the driveway with a shovel, trying to break up the recent ice. Afternoon sun had melted the worst of it at the road end, but the section near the garage was a good two inches thick because it was in shade nearly all the day. They'd talked about regrading this part of the driveway because it drained so poorly, but once the snow disappeared each year, so did their intentions, especially when they thought of the expense.

"I'm going to New York!" she exclaimed, hugging her arms around her torso to stay warm. She explained what had happened.

"Man, that's great," he said, leaning on the shovel. His cheeks were flame-red from the cold, his eyes shining. He loved this, she thought again. The cold springs, the snowy winters, the mountains, the isolation. The late-angling sun painted a pink thread in the darkening sky, visible beyond their neighbors' houses. It served to remind her that life glowed beyond that horizon.

If he finds a job here, we'll never leave. He can't find a job.

It hit her hard, this realization. She wanted to leave; she wanted him to support them. But if he got a job here, they wouldn't leave. Elation left her, replaced by confusion and yearning. What had she been thinking, pleading with him to find a job? No, she did want that, but one farther south. She'd have to add that to her plea. But one didn't just plead at the drop of a hat. It had to rise from the gut. Otherwise, it would be nagging.

"It could mean the beginning of something big," she said, just as much to herself as to him. Yes, a new direction in her writing career. A big seller. He wouldn't have to get a job, after all, and they could move. Because if she were making so much money, he would follow her anywhere, right? Her teeth chattered in the cold, her breath frosting in the approaching twilight.

"You better go in," he said, laughing, "before you freeze your ass off. We can celebrate."

Warming up a few moments later in front of her computer, she found congratulatory emails from her writing pals. But Jackie's was shadowed by distressing news.

Grill this agent on subsidiary rights. Just found out my agent dropped the ball on film interest in my first book. She never sent the manuscript to somebody who was interested. Just like what happened to you. Only found out when that fellow contacted me directly about book three in that series. She tried to cover it by telling me everybody in Hollywood is a snake anyway.

Marie's response: *I think we know who the snake is here. Book agents don't like film and TV options all that much. It's not big money up front for them and few options actually make it to silver screen for the big payoff.*

Kate's comment: *Well, one way to ensure nothing gets made into film is not to submit to film producers.*

Jackie: *Lesson learned. Tell me how this Ranier is, Kate. Maybe I'll be in the agent hunt again soon, too.*

That evening, Kate pretended it was spring. She let the dark hide the remaining snow and ice, and she put daffodils she'd bought at the grocery store in a vase on the dining room table. Kate loved the fall and the spring, the transition seasons, the time when things were on the move. It was the stasis seasons that depressed her — the long, dreary winter, the oppressively hot summer.

She and Jim enjoyed a candlelit dinner, a spring meal of lamb chops and asparagus and new baby potatoes, served with an Australian merlot.

They sat alone together in their small dining room, eating at a table they'd bought at a second-hand store soon after moving into this house. In the corner of the room was an old utilitarian white cabinet that had been in her mother's kitchen. She'd wanted to redo it for years, maybe paint it red. Like the grading of the driveway, it had remained undone, but mostly because Jim rebelled at the do-over, not wanting to touch what was, to him, a vintage look.

Jim held up his glass in a toast. "To us," he said, almost shyly. "To hanging in there."

She smiled and sipped. And thought: so, Jim had also felt he'd been "hanging in there?" She was moody at times, mercurial. She was…not exactly the woman he'd married. Was he the man she'd married? No, neither of them were the same. They were both beaten down, in a way. They'd allowed themselves to become that way.

"To New York," she now toasted, smiling at Jim, "and new beginnings."

New beginnings. Maybe this, at last, would be one.

The day of the appointment dawned gray and damp. Jim surprised her by waking up early and fixing coffee, telling her he knew it was a big day, and that she was nervous. But he assured her she had nothing to fear — *you're a terrific writer, honey, and you have the fans to prove it.*

If anything, that made her more nervous. Ranier knew she wrote genre, but Kate had not gone into a lot of detail on it, except to rattle off some sales numbers from her last royalty statement. She didn't want Ranier taking her on because of those numbers. She wanted an agent who truly appreciated her as a writer filled with potential.

She labored over what to wear, wanting to put on the well-fitting cream-colored pantsuit that made her feel sophisticated and slim but too afraid she'd not be able to keep it clean all day. Instead, she opted for older black slacks, a red silk camp shirt and black cotton jacket that made her feel like a nun in civvies. She hoped her sparkly gold jewelry would somehow move her into the hip category, but ultimately decided it made her go from nun to matron but still nowhere near the frontier of creative artist. Oh, well. Maybe she'd come off as an Emily Dickenson type.

The train station was a mere fifteen minutes' away — they lived in the town with one of the two rail lines south in the state. After the usual pre-travel jitters, she kissed Jim goodbye and boarded, settling into a comfortable seat, watching the state slide away, and eventually the smooth, uncaring Hudson glimmered by, still packed with ice upstate, flowing more freely as they neared the city and its intimidating skyline.

A little after noon, she finally disembarked, hurrying with the crowds up to the main part of the station. Becky said she'd meet her near the restrooms, and Kate searched the sea of faces, worried they'd miss each other, her hand curling around her cell phone to give a call, when she saw her! Her sister was taller by an inch, and her face more angular, more "sophisticated," Kate thought, and she looked fabulous in leather jacket and designer jeans. Just like Becky to know that dressing down might be better than dressing up. Kate instantly regretted not thinking the same way.

They hugged.

"Only been here a few minutes. My train was delayed twice," Becky complained. "Thought I was going to have to text you."

And off they went. They walked out toward Madison Square Garden where the taxi queue would be, and Kate was so glad she'd asked her sister to come. They gabbed about everything, consequential and not so much—from Bob's back problems to Jim's job problems to Becky's girls' college and work problems to what to do with leftover squash. They talked in the taxi line, in the taxi, and on the short walk to the agency office. It seemed as if the importance of the day was sandwiched into the free spots when they had to pause for air.

By now, Kate was reasonably relaxed, even if she dreaded the thought of the elevator ride. She hated elevators, anything closed in, and the office was on the eighth floor.

"She knows I'm coming?" Becky asked once they were n the space and had pushed the floor button.

"Yes, I told her I was in New York with you sightseeing."

"I'll be quiet."

Kate laughed. "You can pretend you're a mute."

"Not that quiet." She shrugged. "Besides, how would I be able to sing your praises if I'm mute? Maybe I'll pretend I'm Russian," she said, rolling her r's with great effect. "That should add some panache."

"What if she speaks Russian?"

"Then I'm hosed."

"Besides, how could you be Russian if I'm not? We're sisters."

"I was adopted?"

The elevator doors opened, and they exited into a short hallway. It was as if they'd entered a church, both reverently silent as they approached the door to the Inner Sanctum.

Through softly closing doors, into the office, and then Kate gave her name to the receptionist who, Kate noted, looked ultrachic in embroidered jacket and bangly earrings, tight hair pulled away from ebony skin.

"This was F. Scott Fitzgerald's agency," Kate whispered to Becky, even though she'd told her a half dozen times already.

"Same office?" Becky asked, looking around at the floor-to-ceiling bookcases crammed with tomes.

"Very same one," the receptionist said lightly from her nearby desk.

The very same one. A temple of books. It smelled like paper. Kate breathed deeply, trying to imagine him coming here, worrying if he'd get a good enough advance to support his rich life with Zelda, meeting with his agent, dragging himself up the stairs, puffing on a smoke. No...did they have an elevator back then? Of course they did. Elevators were invented...well, they had to have been invented before skyscrapers, certainly for buildings with eight floors.

Kate tried to relax, but as every minute ticked by, she became more...disappointed. The office began to lose its cachet. The carpet looked new but shabby. Surely there wouldn't have been wall-to-wall carpet back in the Twenties. The bookcases themselves looked to be particle-board. The art on the walls was...well, a bit cheesy, like awful paintings hung in hotels that no one would want to steal. And Ranier was running late, according to Cool Sophisticated Receptionist. Kate wondered if she was a writer, too, just waiting for her chance. Was she typing notes or working on her own manuscript?

Becky pretended nonchalance, flipping through her phone, answering emails and texts.

Twenty minutes after the appointment time, the receptionist picked up the phone in response to some unseen cue, then ushered Kate and Becky back into Ranier's private office. Another feast of books, not just on shelves but on a table, displayed as if for sale.

"That's one of my clients," Ranier said, smiling, as she pointed to the table where four paperbacks sat, cover out. Kate vaguely recognized them as romancey in tone, if not outright genre. Romance — she represented romance? No, couldn't be. This unsettled Kate.

Ranier was just as cool and hip as the receptionist — no, more so. She wore jeans and riding boots that looked scuffed and worn, not fashion statements. Rail thin, she sported a gauzy pink long-sleeved top that clung to her figure and stayed tucked in to her hip-hugging slacks. Slung over the back of her chair was a brown denim jacket, and her hair was a dirty blond shade, carelessly bundled into a knot at the nape of her neck. She looked wealthy and privileged, as if she didn't need to care what people thought of her, which made Kate want Ranier to care about her.

Kate introduced Becky who, until this moment, had seemed to Kate to be dressed appropriately, even elegantly casual. But now she felt they both looked like bumpkins, but not the colorful kinds that populated earthy stories filled with common-sense wisdom. No, the kinds late-night comics made fun of, the kind that appeared in People of Walmart viral videos.

Ranier urged them to sit and began by complimenting Kate's writing. It made Kate uncomfortable, though, because it seemed false, off, as if Ranier were just trying to butter her up. Ranier asked her what, besides the coming-of-age story she'd rejected, Kate was working on. Kate said she'd been thinking of doing a retelling of *Jane Eyre*, one of her favorites.

"Oh, yes. Wonderful book."

"I've loved it since—"

"The reunion of the husband and wife, wonderful scene."

Kate fell silent.

Ranier leaned forward. "May I see the papers?"

The Rutherford papers—of course. She pulled from her tote bag—a canvas tote, not even a briefcase or some smart leather bag, really, it felt so hickish—and, with some apprehension, handed them over. For a long few minutes, Ranier looked at them, hardly saying a word. Her face registered delight, which made Kate feel comfortable at last, accepted, to have brought this discovery to Ranier's attention. She looked up, peering at Kate over reading glasses.

"Do you mind if I have a copy made?"

"No, go right ahead."

She left immediately, presumably to give the papers to the novel-writing receptionist.

"Nice office," Becky whispered while Ranier was out.

"Mmm," Kate said, smile plastered on her face, feeling as if she had to hide her disappointment from her sister, as if she had to hide from Becky how she'd been impressed by particle-board bookcases and old carpeting just because it covered the floor F. Scott Fitzgerald had walked on.

When Ranier returned, it was with a stranger, a "Miss Angela Somebody," who had stopped in to sign some contracts. While Becky and Kate sat quietly, waiting, this Angela jabbered away with Ranier about New York things as she flipped through page after endless page of a book contract.

Part of Kate rebelled, thinking it was rude. But another part reasoned that they had to wait for the receptionist to make copies anyway, so what did she have to complain about, really? She didn't have a specific book to pitch to her, since Ranier was passing on the *Stillwater* novel, nothing beyond what she'd talked about just now.

Finally, the signing was done, and at that moment the receptionist appeared, two stacks of papers in hand. Ranier gave Kate her originals back. This seemed to be the signal for the meeting to wrap up, so they only talked for a few more minutes. When Kate noticed her looking at her watch, she said they had to be going.

"Send me that manuscript when you finish it," Ranier said, not bothering to walk them to the reception area.

Later, Becky said over lunch, "Rochester didn't reunite with his wife. You know, in *Jane Eyre*. Crazy Bertha dies in the fire."

"I know," Kate murmured. "She must have confused it with another book. Or maybe was thinking of Jane?" Or did she not remember — did it matter? It would have mattered had Kate made that fumble, but with Ranier...even she assumed the woman knew literature. "But wasn't it exciting to be there — to be in that office?"

Of course it had been.

"She had on an odd perfume," Becky said. "Smelled like gin."

"You think she drinks?" Kate hadn't picked up on that at all.

"No. I mean her perfume smelled, oh, like juniper or something. Something expensive."

At that, Kate snickered. "Like gin."

"Top-flight gin."

"Makes me want a martini."

But she didn't order one. The menus they perused were odd. Kate's didn't have any prices on it. How were they to know? Kate had picked out the place after looking it up in an AAA guidebook. Five stars.

Kate was on a budget, and she'd planned on treating Becky, she insisted on it. So she chose what she thought would be inexpensive — chicken salad — placing the order with a waiter who seemed bored to write down what they wanted.

And she didn't remember a single thing about the rest of the lunch, whether it was good, what it cost. All she could think about was that she'd been in the office where he'd tread.

So what if Ranier Thomason wore perfume that smelled like gin? So what if the receptionist was too cool for school? So what if the carpet was new and ugly? Underneath it, the wood floors he'd trod were still there, the soul was still there. Surely that meant something, that Kate, too, was a good writer, to be allowed in that sacred place, to walk where he'd walked?

The problem with gaining entry to the Inner Sanctum was that the door was on an automatic spring that closed quickly and silently. Kate had no follow-up planned. Every time she sat down to tinker with another story, one that Ranier might take on, other tales called out to her. Or she'd end up emailing Marie and Jackie instead. She'd told them about Ranier, a difficult note to write because she felt insincere in describing the agent and the experience. She wanted it to be more than it had been. She was able to say with honesty that she didn't think Ranier would be right for Jackie. She didn't handle YA, as far as Kate could tell. They both cheered her on, keeping their fingers crossed that Ranier was the agent who would make a difference for her.

Finally, procrastination excuses checked off, she settled in to write. She had to finish *Wishful Thinking* for Alice—after Kate had sketched out the rest of the story, Alice was so in love with it now that she'd pushed up the publication date when another book was delayed. Oh, yes, Kate had a contract now for the book. She'd toyed with the idea of having Ranier negotiate it for her, but ultimately balked at handing over fifteen percent of the deal to a woman who'd probably do no more than read the danged thing before sending it on to Kate for her signature. Kate now had to finish writing the book in three months' time—and that included revisions Alice would surely ask for.

On top of that, the Rutherford papers kept calling out to Kate. She wanted to finish typing them so she could begin an essay or paper of some sort on them. She'd talked to someone at a local college, an English professor, who was very interested in co-writing something with her.

And then, there was Jim. He hadn't — wouldn't — give up his "painting." Every afternoon, into the evening, he was down there, whistling, listening to CDs — old Moody Blues songs, some Brad Paisley, Norah Jones, Frank Sinatra, Ravel — it drove her crazy, even when she liked the sounds. It drove her crazy because he thought he was "working."

Where were his attempts at finding a real job? She asked him occasionally, and his responses were murky at best. First, he assured her that her latest effort would sell, and they'd be back on easy street again. And then, he'd smile and say, "And if that doesn't work out, I'll grab anything. I'm still young, eager, got plenty of energy!" This is when she finally had the courage to say she'd like it if he looked for something in Maryland. He'd stared, open-mouthed, clearly surprised by this new demand.

"You really want to go back?" he'd said in a half voice as they lay in bed one night. She'd talked about it — hadn't he listened? Or had she been too vague, too "metaphorical"? Sometimes, she realized, she was like that with Jim, wanting not to have to ask him to do something, wanting him to make the omelet before she said that's what she desired for breakfast.

"I want nothing more. I want to be closer to Becky. And you'd be near your family. I'm tired of living in the Ice Palace!"

They'd left it unresolved, but voicing her desire to move meant he stopped looking — even if he had been looking at all — for anything in Vermont and focused exclusively on his "art."

Maybe he could get something temporary. Maybe that would save her. Save her from having to write scene after explicit sex scene for *Wishful Thinking*. She'd finally given in and written three. Already, she'd had them do it in Jake's house, on his desk at the office, in the elevator — all as she tried to convince the reader that these two numbskulls were afraid the other didn't care as much as they did, even though they thought about each other every waking moment and talked to their respective sibs endlessly about their desire to find the "right" person, but, darn, it just hadn't worked out! She'd even written a sex scene as a joke, something that was so over the top she'd expected Alice to rein her in, but, no, that was Alice's favorite. She'd gotten a big smiley face icon in her email with that one. She wanted to scream. She could work on the Rutherford paper or the new novel — whatever it happened to be — for Ranier. She could do...what she wanted to do to express herself, instead of this dogged slog just to make money if only Jim would find it in himself to love her as much as he loved being loved by her.

Instead, she stared at the latest missive from Alice:

Darling, these scenes are so fresh, the story so exciting, but now I think it's time to "put another bear in the boat." Maybe put the heroine in jeopardy?

She groaned and pulled up the file on her computer.

Two hours later, she'd forced herself through five pages — only five — of writing. Most of the time she'd spent staring at the screen waiting for Jake or Belinda to tell her what to do. She'd considered two possibilities — Jake has a heart attack or thinks he has one, and Belinda rushes to his side, realizing she loves him, or, Belinda becomes the target of an unknown assailant who creepily stalks her and attempts to do her harm. She'd just nixed the first one—although she had to admit to liking the tender, sexless bedside scenes she could write for her two lovers—and settled on the second, when she couldn't find an ounce more energy to devote to their tale.

Spring was fighting what seemed like a losing battle with winter. Just as the last snow faded, a new storm dumped two more inches. She remembered in these moments loathing Edith Wharton's *Ethan Fromm* for all its refrigerated dreariness. She felt trapped in it. In defiance, she opened her window, letting in a cold blast, but at least it was fresh air. A dog barked, a stereo played. Their stereo. This late afternoon, Jim was bidding farewell to the sun with Nat King Cole, who crooned "There was a boy…" an odd song from an odd movie they'd watched late at night a couple years ago.

She sighed. She didn't feel like fixing dinner. Maybe carryout again? Then she sniffed the air. Charcoal. She looked out into the yard. Jim wasn't painting. He was tending the grill. He was cooking dinner for her—out in the snow!

The ache seeped out of her tense shoulders, and she rolled them back and forth to completely banish the day's stress. Jim caught her gaze from the patio and held up a wineglass—he appeared to have set up a little "café" for them in the yard. She saw the edges of a tablecloth flapping in the wind. She smiled back and pointed upward toward the snow. Jim just grinned and shook his head at her pessimism, pointing under the awning, where they could retreat if need be. She laughed. What a nice surprise, for once!

Before going out to join him, she checked email one last time. Two new ones awaited her—both from agents! One was from a Malcolm Gordon with a small boutique agency in upstate New York, telling her he enjoyed her partial and wanted to read the full. The other was from Ranier. Excited, she quickly opened it, hoping she'd see an offer of representation, a rethinking of Ranier's previous rejection of her novel. Instead, the message was short and troubling:

The Rutherford papers are stunning! Our lawyers say they're public domain material. I'd like to chat about provenance. Can you call tomorrow a.m. at nine?

CHAPTER NINE

THE MARCH OF TIME by Beatrice Rutherford
When Zelda appeared on the scene, it was as if Scott just read her mind, thinking of things to make her happy. Later, I realized it wasn't so much a telepathic communication but an extravagance. If one thing didn't work, he'd try another. Jewelry, an expensive flat, parties — whatever she wanted, he'd get for her, trying to anticipate those desires by buying the store out.

I have to admit it was hard seeing them together. At first, I felt as if she was the least suitable match for him, bringing out all his worst attributes, especially his predilection for drink. I was no Temperance Society worshipper; oh, I'd enjoyed, since leaving home and my Baptist strictures, imbibing with abandon and the mellow communion it invited one in. But I knew when it became your minister and your god, and it seemed cruel to me that she would encourage that kind of conversion.

It made me want to scream at them.

Why, one night I did. They'd been galavanting and drinking at speakeasy after speakeasy, with Scott urging me to come along so I could write down anything he thought he might say and want to use later. And they ended up racing out into the street as cars came by, pulling back at the last second when the automobiles saw them and veered and honked. One even ran over Scott's toe, but he was giggling so much he didn't notice until I pointed out the crushed leather and the darkening spot from oozing blood. Zelda just cackled and dared him to do more. He did, of course. There was a kind of desperate effort to please her, as if he was afraid he'd lose her if he didn't.

No, it wasn't that he was afraid of losing her. I know now he was afraid he was losing what was special about his affection for her, those heady is-she-mine days, those melancholy, dragging, aching, sweating days when he'd pounded out *Paradise* as an antidote to her lost love. I think he realized how much he loved *that*. He wanted to be always falling in love with her. I saw the desperation in his eyes for it, the question — will I get it back? And he wanted it back for practical as well as poetic reasons. You can't write about unrequited love so well when your own love's sitting in your lap, cozy as a kitten. He needed that yearning so he could turn out more books.

It occurred to me at that time that I had something he didn't. I had the memory of a great love untarnished by the humdrum of life, where even a special surprise today can be clouded by yesterday's irritation. Jeremy's death had spared me that. An odd consolation, that was.

And Scott, I discovered, didn't write fiction so much as memoir gussied up like fiction. He couldn't seem to pull a foreign idea from his heart or mind. It was all Zelda, Zelda, *Zelda*. Endlessly fascinating Zelda.

And she was fascinating, I had to admit. She was beautiful — it's a shame, really, how none of the photos of her do her justice. She had a rosebud mouth and intense eyes, golden hair, and a way about her. She couldn't sit still. She was always moving, or giving the impression of moving. Like a butterfly. Get too close when it's still, and the mystery goes right out of it. But there was something frantic about her even then, something that went just a little beyond the frivolity of anyone else in a room. She had to prove she was the death defy-er, the risk taker, the one so uncaring of consequences that she'd die laughing about a prank before backing down. That wasn't normal, even in those wild days, it wasn't normal. I thought for a while that maybe I just was too much a stick-in-the-mud to appreciate her, that I'd not moved far enough away from my unsophisticated roots. But, no, everybody else might have thought she was wild. I knew she was crazy.

At first when she showed up in New York, she looked like the Southern hick she was, and I felt not a kinship but a superiority at last. I'd left the ruffles and bows of Montgomery and Atlanta behind, so I felt free to sneer at hers. She caught up soon enough, though, and everyone wanted to know what she was wearing, how she was doing her hair. I was left in the dust, me with my dark cloche hats that went with practically anything, with my two good dresses and one good skirt.

He'd buy her anything, as I said — a diamond as big as the Ritz — to keep that glow on her. And that, too, bothered me, that he was having to work so hard, turning out story after story and the next novel so fast, just so they could live like royalty. Didn't he see — it was as if he was working in the ad agency again, having to write stuff he had no heart for! She'd trapped him into that!

I became so disturbed by this turn of events in his life that I tried talking to him about it. The girls in the office encouraged me when I complained to them about his change of fortune. They said, Bea, you owe it to him. He treasured your counsel on his writing, didn't he?

Armed with this courage by proxy, I entered the battlefield. I didn't say anything wrong or bad about her. I knew that wouldn't go over. But I tried to get him to remember how much he'd wanted a different life from the ad agency, how much he'd wanted to be a writer people remembered, and how he couldn't do that if he was always trying to make a buck. He laughed, patted my hand, said, "Well, now, Bea, you are a wonderful caretaker for me, aren't you?" And he proceeded to tell me how he wanted to hire me at the same wage I was making at the advertising agency to handle his and Zelda's typing and correspondence and such. I told him I'd think about it.

And I did. I thought about it for a good long month. Not that it mattered—he was in such a stupor with her that he barely remembered from day to day what he'd promised a moment ago. For a while I thought I should just pull away from the two of them. They were bad influences. I'd nearly been hauled into a copper's net one night at a speakeasy, barely making it away when they were long down the alley and around the corner.

Home no longer had any appeal for me. I'd feel sick thinking about heading there again, to that creep of time and infernal boredom. Besides, I'd acquired some habits I knew would displease my mama. Better she didn't see them firsthand. So I decided to go back to Madame Solinsky, maybe see my way to that "minor career" she'd talked about. I started studying once a week, and I enjoyed it, except for the stuffiness of the whole business. Why, I remember sitting in her parlor, music in my lap, waiting for my lesson, when another student showed up early, a young, eager thing with red-brown hair, in a suit I would have had to work half a year to pay for, and she talked to me about some Grand Tour she'd just returned from.

European churches had sparked her interest, and she'd stopped in one after another to play the organ because that was her instrument, too, not just "the voice." As she described each one in more glowing terms, I felt this unrelenting urge to laugh. I know it was wrong to feel that way, but, really, she talked about these churches and organs as if they held the key to life itself and if I'd but listen I'd get a glimmer of their greatness — the buildings, that is, not the spirit that was supposed to have moved the builders. It all seemed so meaningless to me. I thought of Jeremy and his dying over there. Heck of a lot of good those churches did him.

That's where I was at that moment in my life, as "sophisticated" as Daisy Buchanan, rejecting tenderness, replacing it with cynicism.

I had no passport to her world, so it was as alien as a fiction, the kind I didn't read, and she a character I didn't want to know.

Later, I regretted this, feeling guilty about how judgmental I'd been. She couldn't help into what kind of family she'd been born any more than I could. And someone had cared enough to build all those organs. One more thing I should know more about.

But I'd learn a thing or two about Europe soon enough. When Scott asked me to go with them, I couldn't turn it down. Free passage — who could say no to that? I wrote my mother, telling her of this wonderful new "opportunity," and gave my notice at the ad agency. I was still wise enough to have saved a few dollars. I figured I'd take this trip as a well-deserved vacation at the very least, making sure I had enough money to return home on my own if need be.

How glad I was that I packed my bags and went! Not only did I get to see a bit of Europe — thinking on my poor Jeremy's feet treading that same ground — but I was privileged to be taken on a far more important and moving journey, as well. It was in Europe that Scott was writing *Gatsby*, and I typed the pages, ever more excited with each passing day.

CHAPTER TEN

BEATRICE DIDN'T WANT to go home, but Kate could think of little else as she took one antacid pill after another, one ibuprofen after another.

She was a ball of worry after the Ranier and Malcolm Gordon emails, wondering what to do, whether she was on the verge of great new things or the usual disappointments. She tossed and turned so much in bed, Jim suggested she just get up and read.

But she couldn't read. She made herself a cup of cocoa, wishing Jim would have gotten up with her, made the hot chocolate, comforted her, talked her through her doubts and fears. He'd done that in the past, at the start of her writing career, when she'd been afraid to give talks at libraries and bookstores. He'd encouraged her to practice and listened to the same little speech over and over to help her grow in confidence.

She sat in her cold, lonely office, peering into the frosty spring night.

౭ఎ౼ఌఄ

Before she'd met Jim, Kate had dated several guys and had had two serious relationships. One was a high school love, a guy who'd been her first crush, Gary. Kind of artsy—he was in the school plays—but also a science nerd — he went on to engineering school, she'd heard — he'd broken her heart by cheating on her in senior year. Then, after a glorious summer of on-again, off-again dating filled with the excitement of knowing but not knowing if things would work out, he had declared his love for her.

Everyone had assumed they'd get married. He'd given her a promise ring, a black onyx with diamond chip in the center, and he'd even bought a few acres of property with some savings from jobs he'd held over the years, paying the mortgage on the plot by working at an engineering firm when he started college. That's where they were going to build their house and live together.

But then she'd met Griffin. She'd been finishing her third semester at the community college and had felt restless. She'd wanted to write. She'd seen an advertisement for a weekend workshop at Hopkins on creative writing, and she'd signed up, sending in a short story to be critiqued by the other students.

The workshop had ended up being a bust, taught by some lame fourth-rate short story writer, an adjunct at some Midwestern college, who didn't seem to understand that folks like her expected something when they paid hard-earned money for it. He'd treated the workshop as a lark, talking a lot about himself at the beginning of the day and doing little to steer discussion in any meaningful way. She'd felt disappointed, cheated.

But at least she'd met Griffin in it. He'd immediately asked her out to coffee, telling her he'd enjoyed her story — which went a long way to softening the anger she'd felt when hers had been the last one to be critiqued, when everyone in the class was eager to leave because Mr. Hot Shot Adjunct Prof hadn't managed the time well. Hardly anyone had said a word about her story, neither good nor bad. That had pinched. It felt worse than the harsh criticism others had received. At least they'd merited comments.

Over coffee, Griffin had explained to her what he'd enjoyed and what he thought she could improve. "Be more specific," he'd said. "Don't just say Sally's afraid. Tell us if she's cold, hot, faint, wide-eyed...." And he had reached for her hand, which had immediately made her warm with blush.

Griffin – blond and long-haired. Leather jackets and expensive jeans. And, despite his parents' wealth, he didn't go to college. He lived in Roland Park, in a big sprawling house that she was only in when no one else was around. Later, she realized his family had probably urged him to take the Hopkins workshop to ignite an interest in higher education. But he insisted he was going to be a writer, and you didn't learn that in a classroom.

Griffin never introduced her to his family. He belittled her own more modest background. Not overtly, of course. But he did tell her his friends didn't think she was "in his league." And he wondered why she insisted on wearing polyester slacks to the movies, the same clothes she wore to work in the drugstore on the weekends. She hadn't thought much about it, had only picked them out because they worked with a top she loved and had paid good money for.

After Griffin, she became acutely aware of class distinctions. She'd known they existed, but she hadn't realized their effect. She'd thought of them only in terms of mean people she didn't like. She hadn't realized people she did like could harbor such feelings.

After Griffin, she began to see the world in terms of old and new, moneyed or not. Even those within her own social sphere were subjected to this analysis.

Highlandtown had ethnic chic, even if it was working-class. Hamilton was an older suburb, poor but with cachet. Rosedale and Dundalk, newer and not cool. Towson—moneyed and "in," even if you happened to have lived there before house values went up.

She broke up with Gary only after she started dating Griffin. Maybe that's what had made the attraction even more electric, knowing she was having an illicit affair. She rationalized it, of course, remembering Gary's own infidelity to her. But that didn't do much to assuage her conscience when she let Gary know she wanted to end things. He asked her right away if there was someone else, and she didn't lie. And then he asked her if she'd been seeing him while they were together, and....it was horrible. Messy and sad and cruel. She felt cruel, too, suddenly realizing she'd stayed with Gary for far too long, not really loving him, being incredibly bored with him and his friends. But he'd been her first love, and she'd felt she was betraying herself by not staying with him.

Her affair with Griffin didn't even last until the New Year. He broke off with her right after Christmas, and she had never in her life at that time—with the exception of the moment she'd heard her father had died—felt so low. In her romantic dreams, she'd imagined that somehow they'd make it work, they'd build a bridge between his sophisticated upbringing and her cheap and tawdry one—for that's how he'd made her feel about it. He'd told her he thought things weren't working out, he wanted space, he wanted freedom, blah blah blah. She cried all night. She even called him and begged him to give them one more chance. And then, as weeks went by, reality cascaded over her like icy rain. She realized he had gone to great lengths at times not to introduce her to his family, that it wasn't just happenstance that had kept them out of each other's way. He'd not even introduced her to their maid! In fact, the one time Kate had run into the woman, she'd had the distinct impression the maid didn't think much of her.

She'd met Jim the following spring at a college mixer, an end-of-year costume party. She'd dressed as a flapper—quick and easy getup, but it was all she could put together on short notice, and she felt like looking pretty—and he'd attended wearing an old doughboy outfit, something moth-eaten from some old relative's closet. They'd danced together because they'd both thought it "essential" that two costumes from the same era be sociable even if they themselves weren't inclined to be. And they'd discovered they were both headed to Towson the next year to finish their degrees. He'd only been living in Maryland because he'd taken a job at a relative's construction business while he went to school.

At first, she wasn't attracted to him. He was thin, almost scrawny then, and he seemed nervous. He had a silly goatee and small eyes. She felt she was doing him a favor, bestowing her attention on him. But he was so…nice. He made sure she was cared for. He got her a drink. He drove her home, because he himself had refrained from over-imbibing. And he asked her out.

He alone among her dates introduced her to his family—mother and father both down from Jersey for a weekend. He'd seemed proud of them and of her. And that had impressed her when so many of her crowd seemed to subscribe to the notion that one should hide one's parents since they were likely to embarrass you.

He'd been eager to meet her family, too, and that had felt liberating. With Griffin, she'd at least subconsciously felt ashamed of them. Jim, with his sweet nature, his quiet self-confidence, made her feel comfortable with who she was and where she came from.

❧❧

Well, if she couldn't sleep and couldn't read, she'd work. Maybe if *Wishful Thinking* sold well, at least it would hasten their journey south. She wouldn't think about Jim's efforts at painting, at finding a job...or not.

She wished...she wished he'd be more as Beatrice had described Scott, eager to anticipate his beloved's needs, not seeming to need cues or words, just knowing. Knowing what would please her. And if he didn't, he'd try anything. Why couldn't Jim be as romantic, as devoted?

She was a strong woman, yes. She didn't believe in fairy tales. But sometimes she really wanted him to know what was wrong and rush in to save her, to make it right.

CHAPTER ELEVEN

WISHFUL THINKING – CHAPTER ELEVEN
He phoned her at ten and still heard the voice mail. Damn. He flipped on the news. They were lovers, he reminded himself, nothing more. She had the right to be out.

Lovers. Surely there was a better word. That morning in the shower just a week ago...and later on the bed. He'd blown off the whole day of work, and she'd been just as truant, giving in to staying with him that night. They'd explored every inch of their bodies, and if either had thought that the consummation of their hunger would lead to disappointment, they were wrong. It led to more hunger. When he awoke, he felt her hand brushing him in the night, ready to stroke passion alive. When he awoke at the crack of dawn, her eyes fluttered and her mouth crept into a smile that meant "more."

God, he burned just remembering.

He'd had other women. He'd had affairs. He was no virgin schoolboy in the throes of first lust. He'd never had anything like this.

They'd gone on the "date" with Chris and his gal, but throughout it, their stares at each other — nanoseconds of connection — had ignited such heat that Chris had joked they should "get a room." They'd gone back to his room, of course, that evening, repeating the whole exquisite experience.

And he didn't know what to do with it, how to keep it, whether he should try, what she wanted, needed. Where did presumption begin and thoughtfulness end?

As images of a Middle Eastern conflict floated across the screen, he decided to call it a night and try her in the morning. *You're a grown-up, Jake,* he told himself. *Act like one.*

The next story stopped him.

"After a second shooting aimed at Mayor Payton Barstow, mayors around the country are beefing up security...." the overly-sincere voice of the news anchor read.

Jake increased the volume and sat bolt upright. His hands started to sweat as he stared at an image of a damaged car, two bullet holes in its left front fender. Then he saw her. Belinda!
She was being helped out of the car by a policeman. Her face was pale as ashes, and he swore he saw her hand tremble. His mouth went dry.

".... Public Affairs Director Belinda Remington was in Barstow's car, and managed to avoid the assassin's attempt with some quick footwork on the brake. Kelly Matchley was on the scene moments after it happened. Kelly?"

The camera panned to a perky young woman with blond hair and plastic smile. "Well, Jarred, Belinda Remington was driving the mayor's car home after a speech by the mayor before the Westside Chamber of Commerce when she saw a dark SUV gaining on her. She slowed to allow it to pass and then saw a gun."

A clip of an earlier interview appeared. Belinda was on screen, looking down, while a microphone was shoved in her face. My god, she was pale. "Belinda," he said under his breath.

"The mayor doesn't use a driver. He usually drives himself. But I offered...." she said, and he had to smile — she was still doing her job, taking the opportunity to paint the mayor as a man of the people. "The windows of Payton's car are dark," she said. "So they probably thought it was the mayor." But Jake could tell she was trying to convince herself, not the newswoman.

As the camera panned back, Jake saw a dark stain on Belinda's pants. She'd been hurt! He grabbed his phone and redialed her number. Still no answer. Was she in a hospital somewhere? Staying with friends? What if she had gone home and the assailant had followed her?

He stood and started pacing. He wanted to go to her, to get on the road to New Jersey. He didn't even know her address. What if she tried to reach him in the meantime here on his landline? Did she have his cell? God, he couldn't remember. First order of business when they got together next, he thought grimly, would be to share all phone numbers and addresses. And maybe even those of close friends and relatives. Next of kin.

He paced into the kitchen and poured himself a drink, knowing adrenaline would dull its effect. He punched the redial number to no avail. After finishing his drink, he picked up the phone to try again. As he pulled it into view to repeat his call, it rang.

It was her. Weary and tentative.

"Jake?"

"Belinda! Are you all right? Did he hit you in the leg? Have you seen a doctor? Let me come up there." He gripped the phone tightly, as if he would lose the connection after finally making contact with her.

"I'm fine," she said. "Just a little shaken. I...I...just didn't want you to worry. Sorry about calling so late."

"Belinda, I wish you would...." He stopped because he was afraid she'd feel overwhelmed. He wished she would come stay with him where he could protect her. "I wish you would let me help you."

"Talking is a help. A big help," she said so softly that he almost couldn't hear her. She sounded bone-tired and depressed. "I...I...don't think I handled it very well."

"The news said you used some 'quick footwork.'"

"Yeah. I took my foot off the gas pedal, then slammed it into the brake. I wasn't thinking."

"Whatever you did, it saved your life."

"They must have thought it was Payton. He has special license plates."

"Did you ever mention to the police that you could have been a target of the other shooting?"

"No," she said, breathing out the word. "It seemed kind of....silly."

"Belinda!" The other incident had taken place while she'd been at his place, a shooter who'd targeted the "grip and grin" she'd described. She'd been scheduled to be at that event, but she'd been with him. Thank God.

"Why would someone be after me? It's clearly aimed at Payton. Otherwise..." Her voice tapered off in a fluttery breath. He knew what she was thinking. Otherwise the killer would be after her in other places, like her apartment.

"Belinda," he said very softly but firmly. "I know you can handle this on your own. But it would make me feel immensely better if you let me come to Jersey. Or you came here. Just until things settle down."

He thought he heard a catch in her voice. Then, a sniffle. She was crying. He gritted his teeth.

"No, Jake. I refuse to let you get on the road at this hour. And I'm not going anywhere tonight. I'm dead tired," she said, then laughed nervously. "I guess that's not a good choice of words."

"Belinda…" He had to control his voice. He cleared his throat. "I'm coming to fetch you. You'll stay with me. Please, don't argue. Let me do this for you. For…us."

"Jill, the chief of staff, could come over," she said, as if she hadn't heard him. "Or Connie, my assistant. But they have families. Jake, I'll be all right. Really. I promise." Her voice sounded stronger, but he suspected she was making it sound so for his benefit.

"Belinda, I'm coming. It will take me a few hours, that's all. And then back here…."

He heard her sniffle, and then she uttered a tremulous, "All right."

"Pack your things," he said, filled with grateful confidence.

"My sexy things?" she joked, and he closed his eyes with relief.

"All the sexy things you have," he said. "Even those you aren't sure about."

"Like the footie pajamas."

"Bring them. They won't last long," he countered.

"Okay."

He got her address, quickly made coffee to go and hit the road.

Within a few hours, he was there, and the way she grabbed the lapels of his jacket and showered him with hot kisses, he knew he wasn't leaving that night.

"God, I missed you," she moaned as he nibbled hungrily at her neck and pulled her as close as he could hold her.

"Show me," he groaned.

CHAPTER TWELVE

JIM WAS THE one who gave Kate the courage to take on Ranier. He'd insisted, in their snow-dampened dinner the night before, that she not call the agent back at nine the next day but whenever the hell she felt like it.

Then, in the morning, obviously seeing the worry in her eyes, and, after discovering she'd spent a good part of the night up and working, he asked her, point-blank: "What do you want from Ranier? What do you not want?"

It was the second question that helped the most.

With stunning clarity, it led her to the answer: she didn't want Ranier's representation. Not unless she was calling to say she had an editor dying to buy Kate's work at that moment.

Ranier didn't really "get" her as a writer, not if she represented some romancey novelist—Kate had had a chance to research the author whose books had been so prominently displayed in Ranier's office, and she was a commercial writer, someone whose books had done well, one even hitting a best-seller list. Kate began to see, as she talked things over with Jim, that Ranier might have found her attractive as a potential client because of her romance background, her ability to sell there. She'd reap the commissions from any of those future sales, and how much would she really push Kate's serious stuff? Kate's work in romance would be used to bankroll Ranier's representation of literary authors whose advances and commissions wouldn't keep the lights on.

"What you need is someone who can just negotiate the romance contracts but really push for the literary stuff," Jim told her as he refilled her coffee mug.

"What should I do about the Rutherford papers?" she asked.

"Well, I don't think you should have let her have a copy, but that water's under the bridge." He sat down opposite her at their small kitchen table. "You want some eggs or something?" he asked. When she shook her head no, he went on. "I'd tell her you're publishing a paper related to them, and their provenance will be laid out in that work. Tell her you have a lawyer handling it."

"Or another agent." Malcolm Gordon — he wanted to see more of her stuff. She'd emailed him the full coming-of-age story, but could he help her with the Rutherford material? She mentioned this to Jim.

"Mmm, I don't know if I'd drag another agent into it. You want him excited about you, not this find of yours. Maybe ask his advice after you snag him." He reached across the table and squeezed her hand. "And you will. Just make sure you want him, even if he wants you!"

After breakfast, she shared her Ranier woes with Marie and Jackie, too, and got the usual Agents Suck emails in return. She could have written them herself. But it didn't matter. It only mattered that they understood, just as Jim had.

With Jim's encouragement ringing in her ears, she phoned Malcolm Gordon after showering and changing. She didn't call Ranier. She knew she'd just sent Malcolm her manuscript, but she wanted to talk to him, to get a sense if she should even bother hoping he was right for her.

To her surprise, he took her call. She squared her shoulders and, in a strong, businesslike voice, told him she wanted to chat as he started to read her story.

"I've already read it," he said simply before she had a chance to go through the list of items she'd intended to talk about. "And I like it."

She was speechless. Did this mean he was offering representation?

"Yes?

"It's good, Kate—may I call you Kate? I really enjoyed it."

"But…" She heard it in his voice. There was a "but." There was always a "but." Her shoulders sagged.

"But I'm not sure it will sell."

"It's not commercial enough," she said in a monotone.

"Oh, it's commercial enough. It's accessible but thoughtful. It doesn't stand out enough, though."

"But you could say the same thing about a dozen other best sellers," she said, hating the whiny sound in her voice, but tired of being shut out of the Inner Sanctum.

He was not irritated. Instead, he agreed. "Yes, and each of them has something else that makes them special, usually something about the author. If you were some young thing—"

"I'm not that old!"

He chuckled. "I didn't think you were old. But if you were eighteen or even twenty—my God, with your background, working class, no-name college, you'd be a prodigy, a phenom. Landon's rather a blah name, though."

"My real name's Lazlo," she said, giving her married name. She'd used Landon in her correspondence because it was on all her books. "But my maiden name was Brzneckie."

"Difficult, but possibly good. You might want to use it on your non-romance things. We'll talk about it. Or an editor will advise you once you sell."

Once you sell—she liked the sound of that.

"All those things you mentioned—working-class background, no-name college—they're still true, except for being a young whipper-snapper," she said softly.

"Mmm...except the romance writing, too."

"What on earth does that have to do with anything? I would think it would make me more attractive, breaking out from that genre."

"It means you're not a discovery. The aristos can't feel special about having found you when thousands of the bourgeoisie have already read you. To them, you're not fresh."

"A tarnished heroine," she murmured, thinking of the conceits of the romance field.

"Not really. It would be better if you were—maybe get arrested?" he joked.

She laughed, despite her disappointment.

"So, you don't think it's worth trying?"

"Oh, I'll try," he said. "I just want to warn you. It's a steep hill. In the meantime, keep writing."

"You're offering representation?"

"I was going to call you, but you beat me to it."

"For the manuscript you read, not one you'll wait for me to write?"

He laughed softly. "That's generally my practice. I don't like to represent things I've not read."

"I—I—" She looked at her list of questions. She imagined what Jim would say if she didn't ask them. Fighting back the urge just to say yes before he changed his mind, she pressed on. "Do you mind if I ask you a few things?"

"Not at all. Shoot."

For nearly a half hour they talked, and, while she didn't like all his answers—how often he actually went to New York to meet with editors, what he thought the market was like for the sweet romances that were her bread and butter—she was reasonably satisfied. After going over the details of his representation contract, which he emailed while she was still on the phone with him, she chewed at her bottom lip. What the hell—

"I have another...issue...I need advice on...." She told him about the Rutherford papers and Ranier's request.

He listened quietly and, after a pause, said, "As soon as you sign and fax back that contract, I represent you. I'll email her about it, telling her she's to send the manuscript back to you."

And that's exactly what he did by noon of that day, copying Kate on the email. He was straightforward but firm. "I'm representing Ms. Landon now, and she would like the manuscript she let you copy, by a Beatrice Rutherford, back as she has other plans for it. You may send it to me and I'll forward it to her. It is her property."

ولى

True to his word, Malcolm Gordon retrieved the Rutherford manuscript from Ranier's office and sent it off to Kate. The process took more than a week, with Malcolm having to nudge Ranier more than once. This troubled Kate for an unknown reason. Maybe it was because, as Becky suggested, Kate was still disappointed that Ranier turned out to be so shallow, and her tardiness with returning the Rutherford manuscript was just a reminder of that disappointment.

Whatever the reason, Kate pushed those thoughts to the back of her mind as she toiled on *Wishful Thinking.* She had to power on through and finish the first draft, including changes Alice had been sending her as she read chapters. Kate didn't usually write this way, giving an editor a chance to look at the book in progress, but somehow they'd established the pattern for this manuscript. Kate suspected Alice wanted to keep a tight rein on the book.

She was so busy, in fact—and maybe, too, so happy with the changing season—milder days came with more frequency now, even if temperatures still hovered around freezing in the mornings and late at night—that Kate didn't even get too bothered about Jim and his job-hunting. Or lack thereof. He'd gone on a few interviews, yes. One to a computer store. One to a software company. Another to a video marketing firm. Form rejections followed in quick order. What was he saying in those interviews anyway? She knew he could be quite charming. Was he deliberately sabotaging himself?

These interviews had been set up before her request for him to search in Maryland, so she should have been happy that none of them came through. Instead, they seemed to feed her suspicion that he wasn't really trying at all. If he couldn't land such easy jobs up here, what hope was there he'd get something in Maryland? At least a job up here could be a nice temporary fix, some extra steady cash they could sock away for moving expenses.

Her confusion meant that her questions and resentments were held at bay; more than anything she wanted to leave. She'd thought that spring approaching would soothe her longing, her *sehnsucht,* but instead it seemed to amplify it. Her sister cheerfully reported on the farmette's quickening in the warm weather there — they were getting ready to put seedlings in for tomatoes and corn, and already daffodils were passing, azaleas ready to bud. The grass in Kate's yard stayed brown, the rhododendron leaves curled in protection against still chilly nights. She often felt like that bush, folding in on herself, refusing to acknowledge the frigid atmosphere, protecting herself from it all the same.

She talked more about this with Jim, even spending a few more dreamy evenings on the kitchen porch steps, still in parkas, describing for him the white house she dreamed of living in, the peaceful, quiet place near some water. Responding to her earlier delight, he'd made dinner there a couple more times, and she'd leaned her head on his strong shoulder as they'd huddled against the encroaching cold night.

He listened patiently, even sympathetically, sometimes adding touches of his own.

"There should be a porch swing," he said one night. "Like the one I got you. Except on an actual porch."

"We could take it with us," she agreed. It was as if they were actually planning the move, and this cheered her, even as her below-the surface anger still simmered.

When Jim came home from his job appointments, he immediately retreated to the basement, cranked up the music and painted. He had a series of paintings now, all in the same "family" as the "Eye of the Peacock," which had reappeared after its brief stay with a downtown gallery owner who, she learned later, had been assessing it. Jim had shared little of that session beyond some comments on how the owner saw "promise" in his work.

Promise? Did Jim know that meant he'd not seen real art, that he was letting him down easy? Kate was no stranger to rejection — she'd dealt with enough agents to know its sugar-coated varieties. Like Jim, she'd at first believed the "shows promise" variety of "no," thinking just a few more tries would have promise fulfilled. Not so. "Shows promise" in her business meant, "I'm not the one to make promises to the likes of you."

Promising art by Jim Lazlo. Unlike Kate, he was using his real name. And she realized, after her chat with Malcolm about her future, that this got under her skin, too. She'd had to hide her name — Brzneckie was too difficult to pronounce, her first agent had suggested, and come up with the Landon moniker after she'd mentioned her married name, Lazlo.

One of Jim's paintings was nothing more than profile figures of a man and woman, the kind you'd find on restroom doors. Actually, Jim had found some being thrown away, picked them up, created stencils, and, well, what could be more obvious? When she pointed this out, he just shrugged and said "It's good enough for Penn Station." Ah, yes, the towering sculpture in front of Baltimore's train station, a gigantic metal version of the same types of figures.

She hated those sculptures! So did many others, who'd critiqued them, made fun of them. But what Jim was doing...it still felt like a mockery of her, not of that other garbage! She sulked, and finally, after snapping one too many times at Jim to be healthy, after more sleepless nights that left her too tired to write in the morning, she folded up her laptop to visit her sister for a week, telling Jim she needed to get away to clear her head, she needed spring.

෨෧෩

And spring she got. Warm baby's breath spring. Sun-dappled spring. Afternoons in Becky's flower garden, sitting on a bench while her sister weeded and mulched, listening to bees begin their relentless buzz, sniffing tulips, admiring with childlike glee the newest blooms each morning, the nips of lilac, the pregnant irises, the shy columbine, and the little chickadees flitting in and out of birdhouses. One morning, she saw blue jays squawking in amicable disagreement. Harbingers of happiness, she exulted! It was as if the whole world were a box she was slowly unwrapping, with layer after layer of color and texture and light, light...*light!*

Despite leaving Vermont so she could be away from Jim and alone with her thoughts, she yearned to share all this with him. Yes, she missed him.

Becky and Bob fed and pampered her, her nieces stopped by for a family dinner. Their references to popular culture made her feel old, though, and she sometimes thought her life in Vermont was akin to being locked in a time capsule, even in this instant internet age. They marked the visit by friending her on Facebook, something she'd been reluctant to initiate, and they assured her their posts would keep her up to speed.

She enjoyed sitting on her sister's quiet front porch listening to crickets hum away the days while she tapped at her story, rushing to do revisions of various scenes Alice had sent her way.

In the middle of her tapping, she received an odd email from Malcolm. Odd because it was a Saturday. Since when did agents work on Saturdays?

Have you seen this, he wrote. Pasted below those words was a short "deal announcement" from Publishers Marketplace, which she'd not been reading in her deadline rush. The deal being announced was Ranier Thomason's six-figure contract with a Random House imprint to release "recently discovered papers of F. Scott Fitzgerald's typist...."

Kate couldn't even read the rest. Words jumped at her, but her vision blurred. "Exciting find," "rush release," "supplemental essays by leading literary stars...."

Her hands shook. She got up, paced the porch. She was alone. Bob and Becky were in their insurance agency office for the morning, handling weekend calls. How she yearned to call Jim, to tell him all about this, to hear his protective indignation overlapping his warm embrace of support!

Instead, she fisted her hands and cried. Again—she was being pushed out. Again! Supplemental essays by leading literary stars—others would be showcased with what she had found! No essay by Kate Landon—or Kate Brznecki—among the bunch! Those papers were her discovery. And she'd planned on doing something with them, publishing them academically, as a scholarly work. She had that interest from the professor. A horrible thought came to her. What if he turned out to be just as bad as Ranier? What if he took all the credit, stole the work from her?

Damn it. Damn it.

She felt played. Ranier Thomason had never been interested in her. She'd seen her as a convenient check from her romance writing, money she'd use to float her handling of "more important" writers, and then she'd stolen the Rutherford papers from her.

No, not stolen. Kate had stupidly, naively handed them over without a protest. She'd wanted to impress Ranier. She'd wanted to be...inside the circle, not standing outside looking in. And what a fool she'd been to think that merely having Ranier relinquish her copy of the papers meant she hadn't made another copy to keep!

Drying her tears, she took a deep breath and walked back to her laptop perch on the front porch. She sat down and wrote back to Malcolm, asking what she could do, what was his advice. She gave him her cell number, saying she was out of town for the weekend.

To her surprise, he called her within a few moments. In his smooth voice, he gave her the bad news first.

"If they're in the public domain, they're in the public domain," he said. She was glad he didn't remind her that she'd made a mistake giving the papers to Ranier in the first place.

"But...but I was going to do something with them," she murmured. Or maybe, it was what they were going to do for her that mattered. They were to have been her ticket to literary greatness, to being taken seriously. Maybe it was egotistical, self-centered to think that way, and she'd just been caught in a trap of her own making.

There was no key to literary greatness. There was only the story, telling the story. Telling the story her way, in her voice.

"You're sure they're real?" he asked. "Not fiction?"

"I have no idea if they're real. I think they are, but...I mean, I haven't carbon dated them or anything like that," she said. What if they were fiction, someone's flight of fancy, the beginning of a novel…? What a lovely novel it would be, too. If she wrote it, she already thought of how it would end.

"Malcolm," she said, as the ideas formed, "I was thinking of using them for a novel, as a foundation for one." She made it sound like a well-formed plan, when it had been but a fleeting thought. Her heart raced, her breath came fast as the moment of epiphany lit her. Sometimes, when retyping the papers, she'd thought of rewriting Beatrice's story, giving it a happy ending. She'd been so blue typing the pages about the Fitzgeralds' stay in Europe, the birth of Scotty, Zelda's descent into madness. Oh, how she'd longed to change those scenes. She'd started imagining how different their lives could have been. Beatrice herself had inspired her to think that way. "Most of all, I'd wanted them to be happy," she had written. And Kate felt the same way.

"What do you mean?" Malcolm urged.

Shyly, she stammered out her desire to redo their tale so it ended in a version of the romance HEA — happily ever after.

"Oh, not the both of them swooning in each other's arms," Kate said, thinking of how Alice would have had her write it. "But something where Zelda gets better, at least enough to function, and maybe even prosper, and then she ends up kind of holding things together for Scott, whose own health is starting to crumble…"

There was a pause. She thought she sounded silly, and he was trying to figure out how not to sound appalled, how to tell her it "showed promise."

Instead, he gushed: "How long would it take you to write that?"

"I don't know. I have to finish *Wishful Thinking.*" She explained where she was in that project, feeding Alice finished chapters so they could revise as she went along.

"How long would it take for you to do up a proposal, maybe a sample chapter — the ones you'd write, not Rutherford's? And a decent synopsis."

"I don't know. A week maybe." If she wrote around the clock.

"What about by Monday?"

Monday! She had to...she looked down at her laptop, the manuscript open before her. If she put it aside, lost a day...it was just a day. It would still be there when she returned to it on Monday. And if she worked double-time. And this was what she wanted, writing Beatrice's story, Zelda's story, not Belinda and Jake's...wasn't it?

"I could try...."

"I'll research this Beatrice Rutherford to make sure the stuff really is in the public domain. You send me what you have by Monday morning. If I like it, we'll try to get it published. At the least, it will stop Ranier."

"How?"

"She can't publish something not in the public domain."

"But this is. I mean the first part of it is."

"You assume it is. You just said you don't know for sure. You were going to investigate that further when you showed the pages to her originally. If it is, your new story isn't. And that's the angle I'll use."

She sat back, a smile lifting her lips. Her cheer was short-lived, though, when Malcolm went on, without a pause, giving her bad news.

"While I have you on the phone, Viking passed on *Stillwater Dreams*. So did Atria," he said, mentioning a Simon & Schuster imprint. "I'll forward you the emails."

They popped up on her laptop a few seconds later while Malcolm talked about other possibilities. She skimmed them, snorting with indignation.

"…Ms. Landon is such a talented writer, and this story is so strong and memorable. I read it all in one sitting, eager to get to the end. Her characters are well-drawn, her descriptions so real I thought I was in that time and place. But in the end, the turn of events that leads to the denouement felt too contrived…But I'm sure you'll find someone to snatch this up, and I eagerly await the moment I see it on bookstore shelves."

The second rejection was virtually a copycat of the first.

"I just read the rejects."

"I know, I know…" Malcolm said before she had a chance to comment. "Would be funny if it wasn't so idiotic."

"Um, does her boss know this?"

"You mean that she's eager to go into a bookstore to buy a smash her competitors published but she rejected?"

"I don't get it."

"They're all afraid. They think they can only buy megasellers. They think if something doesn't shout best seller, they can't risk taking it on."

"But she thinks it will be a good seller, at least. How do they know they'll be best sellers?"

"Exactly. If they counted up how many just sell decently, they'd realize what a crapshoot getting a best seller is, and they'd buy what they like."

"Which is why they were hired in the first place, right? To use their judgment."

"One would think so." He chuckled. "You'd think the fact that she read the whole thing would tell her something. They rarely read the whole thing."

"I suspected that."

"Pity them," he said. "They all start work thinking the publisher wants them for their literary judgment, their knowledge of fiction, their 'eye.' And they find out they're cogs in a wheel. No one has responsibility for success or failure. If a book does poorly, it's marketing's fault, the team's fault, the salesmen's fault, even readers' fault. If it does well, they all pat themselves on the back. No one is punished or lauded sufficiently to make a difference in how it all works.

"That cheers me," she murmured sarcastically.

"Onward!" he said, and she knew the conversation was over. For once, she didn't feel like lingering on the phone, didn't need that connection to bolster her confidence or boost her morale. She had too much to do.

≈

She worked around the clock the next day, on fire to get something to Malcolm he could use. But she deleted more than she wrote, feeling her pretend story no match for Beatrice Rutherford's own tale.

She spent some time regaling Jackie and Marie with the latest news. Jackie lifted her spirits considerably with an "interpretation" of the rejection notes she'd just received:

I'm sorry I have to pass but my assistant read the manuscript before she lost it and I'm mad at my boss anyway or maybe the board of directors, I was sleeping with the boss, though, and he ended it when his wife found out, so then I wanted to really screw him, if you know what I mean, so I'm rejecting anything that looks like it will sell more than fifty percent of its print run because that's the magic number in this business, and when he sees your book doing well published by a competitor I can tell him he doesn't pay us enough to make good decisions. I hate publishing and am becoming a Buddhist monk.

Marie chimed in with her own version: *The team made me do it. Marketing and sales and the other editors. They hypnotized me. I am now quacking like a duck every time someone says or writes vampire.*

But sweet-natured Jackie did point out, just as Malcolm had, how editors were probably just as much a victim as anyone else in the business.

Can you imagine – they get hired, all excited with their spanking new degrees in literature or creative writing or writing seminars from Smith, Wellesley, Yale, thinking their corporate bosses want them to actually think, only to find out that their judgment hardly matters. Or doesn't really matter at all. All that matters is what marketing or sales or half-baked numbers say. They don't have a chance. They're just as trapped as we are.

Marketing, Marie wrote back — *the people who brought us New Coke.*

Jackie: *No, it's worse in publishing. There, the marketing team would probably tell you the reason Coke sells so well is because it's in red cans.*

Marie: *Write more red cans!*

Jackie: *Red cans and vampires!*

Marie: *Fifty shades of red cans!*

Continuing on a more serious note, Jackie went on to share that she was definitely dumping her agent after getting some leads on better ones. She wasn't going to even give her a chance with a "talk." *I've had talks with her before, and, oddly enough, she promises to pay more attention to my stuff, yet doesn't. I seem to recall having a talk with her before she muffed that film interest.*

Marie urged Jackie to share more of that story that Kate hadn't heard.

She called me on a Friday afternoon after hearing from the film subagent that I had to make a decision on whether I was including other dramatic rights in the sale. I have a cousin with Broadway connections. My cousin was having it read by a producer. I asked her if she would call the Broadway producer for me to tell him we had this film interest, blah blah blah. I figured an agent calling is better than the author calling. She wouldn't do it. Said she'd earned her few hundred bucks for this already. And then she told me I had to get a decision back to her by five, eastern time, even though the Hollywood folks would be open for three more hours. She just wanted to wash her hands of it.

Kate cringed. *Oh, Jackie, that's awful. She needs to go. It shouldn't matter that the film option commission is so small. It can lead to bigger things.*

Jackie: *I said that, too. She said that editors hear about film options all the time and roll their eyes.*

And then Marie chimed in with her own bad news—a spate of low-star reviews on Goodreads. *I think I ticked off someone in the Goodreads compound. Gave a so-so review to a best seller, and a pack of reviewing wolves decided to avenge their leader.*

Jackie: *Cheer up. Remember that stinker novel I told you about a few months ago?*

Kate: *The one where you were hoping the author would kill the protagonist and end your misery?*

Jackie: *Yeah – it's up on Goodreads with something like ninety-eight ratings and an average of 4.8 stars. Pride and Prejudice doesn't get that many.*

Kate: *The Great Gatsby doesn't get that many.*

Marie: *Farewell to Arms doesn't get that many.*

Kate: *Maybe we should write an article about this.*

Jackie: *Anonymously.*

Kate: *They'd still find us.*

Marie: *With their one-star torches blazing.*

As they emailed each other, Kate received another rejection…this one from an agent she'd forgotten she'd queried before landing Malcolm. She immediately forwarded the note to her two writing pales.

Kate: *Hot off the press….*

Dear Author,

Well, I'm sorry to have to report that after over two decades in this business, paying careful attention to every note I get from authors, I have had to change my ways and finally recognize that a new time has come upon us all. Before email, my query load was manageable. Now I receive so many that I'd have to spend every waking hour doing nothing else but read and respond to them. I'm sorry, I really can't standing doing this. I know that writing a book is an immense amount of work, the best work in the world. And I swear, I'm in complete sympathy with your passion. We do still read queries, but we're only responding personally to those whose work we're interested in. Please forgive us for this impersonal form note. We hate having to take these Draconian measures, and we're sure there's the perfect representative waiting for you. We wish you all the best in your search.

Jackie: *Good lord, is that a rejection or a pre-rejection?*

Marie: *No, it's a diary entry. It's all about the agent, see? Not about you, Kate. Not.At.All*

Kate: *LOL*

Jackie: *Be thankful. That's one bad piece of writing. If she had offered revision ideas, God help you.*

Becky was a peach, fixing meals, staying out of her hair, not insisting on gab sessions, keeping Bob away, too: "Don't bother Kate—she's on deadline." In the middle of the afternoon, Jim called, and he did seem to want to gab, telling her about some local scandal, mentioning that he saw some crocus blades in the front yard. She didn't say much, and finally he asked if she was still angry at him. They'd not really argued before she left, but he knew why she'd gone away.

She didn't feel like arguing now, so she told him the story of Malcolm's call, Ranier's betrayal, her need to write something fast.

"Not going well?" he asked at the end of her recitation of woes.

"Beatrice is too good, too real."

"Just pretend you are Beatrice," he said. "You know, southern drawl and all." He dropped the "d" in "and" to demonstrate. "Didn't you tell me that you do that with characters? Pretend you're them and talk like them?"

Yes, she had told him that. Sometimes she'd even "interviewed" her characters and been surprised what they'd told her. She was touched he'd remembered.

But Jim remembered a lot of things, she realized. He was quiet, introverted, but he didn't forget things like this. For a crushing moment, she wondered if she needed to trust him more.

Their conversation ended on a warm note. She promised him she'd be on the train on a train in the next few days, and she'd call with the ETA details.

And she turned back to the computer and pretended she was Beatrice, and hell if the words didn't flow from her head to the computer screen, in a rush, as if she were connected, brain to electronic brain, the way she sometimes wished she could be when writing, bypassing the physicality of the act, the translation of idea to thought to word to fingertips typing out sentences....

CHAPTER THIRTEEN

THE MARCH OF TIME by Beatrice Rutherford

Zelda and I ended up becoming friends, a shock as much to me as it was to her, I do reckon…I think the tide turned when I saw how Scott didn't want her doing any writing. That was his bailiwick, he believed. He was the man of the family, the earner. Well, I'd learned a thing or two about women and earning. You couldn't count on a man. He might up and die on you, the way Jeremy had. You had to have something of your own. So I always thought it was a great mercy she was discovering her voice, something that would let her sing to the heavens the way he had. And I must admit that at that time I did begin to weary a bit of his endless examination of their lives, turning them over and over again in his hand as if they were an artifact about to yield the secrets of mankind. It became less romantic and more self-indulgent. I began to think that maybe history was turning a page, and the next page would be written by Zelda, not by Scott.

But this was after things fell apart.

When I first went to Europe with them, there was so much partying and doing anything but work that I was able to get my holiday. At first, it didn't seem like one, until I figured things out. You see, I'd rise each morning, pencil and notepaper at the ready, typewriter, too. And

I'd have myself a nice breakfast of café au lait and French bread or a croissant with whipped honey, feeling as contented as a cat in sunlight. Sometimes at the hotel where we stayed, later at the villa on the Riviera. And I'd wait. And wait. And think about all the places I could be seeing, all the wonderful museums and monuments and boulevards I could be viewing, adding to my education and understanding of the world, resenting each moment my services were not used. When he finally arose and drank his own coffee, red-eyed, slack-jawed, smoking, he often wasn't fit to work. He'd gab a bit at me, talk about his ideas, then wave his hand in the air and say, "come back at three."

I'd come back at three, only to be put off again.

This happened a week or more, and finally I'd had enough and decided I needed to devise my own plans. So I rose one day, had my breakfast, waited until a decent hour, then left a note saying I'd be back at three. Sometimes he was there ready to work, sometimes not. But he never complained.

I saw my bits of Europe that way, even getting out to the place where Jeremy had been killed, or so the Army told me when I was notified. I said a prayer and laid some roses by the roadway. It was all I could do, and it hardly seemed enough. It seemed as though it should be more momentous than it was, this visit to the last patch of earth he'd ever known. And it added to the melancholy of the day that it was so ordinary, with people passing by who didn't know the love of my life had perished on that spot.

The land was still rutted and the trees a mass of stumps with a bit of new growth, and it broke my heart afresh to think of him in such an ugly place breathing his last. I couldn't think about it long, or I'd get to sobbing. I stayed upright and bit my lip and forced my mind through all the prayers I could remember. I'd stopped regular church-going by then. I resolved to get back into it, and eventually, years later, I did.

But in those days—those heady, sun-drenched, holiday days—contentment was the altar at which I worshipped. I was aware of foundations crumbling, to be sure, of their marriage and her sanity drifting, like sand, out to sea. But at that point, I was of a mind to think they were getting what they deserved, even him, who I still adored at least for his talent, or so I convinced myself.

You see, as in the way of things, I had gone from one superlative to another with him. From "best" to "worst" in the blink of an eye. His love of fun was now mere dissipation in my eyes. His desire to please Zelda, a pathetic slavishness. To damnation with them, I thought in my falsely sophisticated way.

Oh, I was very much aching to prove how sophisticated I could be because, for the first time since my marriage—I don't count my girlish admiration of Scott in this same regard—I actually found myself thinking of another man besides Jeremy, a Mr. R. I found myself smitten with him, in fact, a crippled ex-soldier, ex-patriot like us, living on a trust fund in France, sad and handsome and oh, so, pitiable. He walked with a cane, had a moustache that covered some scars around his mouth, spoke French as good as a native, and he played the piano.

I met him at a party, of course, and we'd got to talking about music, you see, and I'd let my usual chip slide from my shoulder, thinking here was a kindred spirit in the land of classless equality. Here was…what Jeremy might have been had he been merely wounded and not killed. A natural nursing instinct first touched me, but it was followed soon enough by less noble sentiments.

He invited me to his fine home. He accompanied me at the piano, and for the first time, I sang as if I really could sing, as if I could be a great singer. I sang French melodies he showed me, things by Gabriel Faure and Claude Debussy, and they just made my heart quiver with their loneliness.

I will not say his name nor give away too much of his circumstances because he was married. His wife was back home in New York, he told me. And, I will confess to nearly succumbing completely to his charm, the only thing ultimately pushing me back not a sense of moral rectitude but rather ego, plain and simple. That willful self-regard that reared its head at just the right moment.

He might have loved me in private, but he was ashamed of me in public. Me with my Southern accent that couldn't seem to get my mouth wrapped around those straight French vowels except in song. Me with my dresses he considered not so chic, even making fun of my best garment, a floral print dress of flowing chiffon that made me feel girlish without being over-frilly and too sweet, or so I thought. But that was precisely its fault, according to him. What, Bea, you're trying to recapture the days of your childhood—are bows and plaited hair next? And he'd laughed, picking up the dress's hem to examine the fabric. I'd spent a week's salary on that dress, and I'd felt pretty in it.

That had brought tears to my eyes. It felt so cruel to mock me like that when he knew I had an artist's soul. He'd seen it on display, after all, when I'd poured my heart into the songs he played. Beatrice, the artist, he liked. Beatrice, the woman, he derided. I noticed how he didn't shower me with the same affection in public as he did in private, that he all but ignored me around others, and it was clear enough — he was ashamed to be seen on the same level with me.

I thank God for my healthy ego, then, since it kept me from straying into shameful adultery. And it was this resistance on my part that also helped feed my hard judgment of Zelda when she wandered into that territory. It took years for me to realize that only my hurt at being mocked saved me from her fate. If R had not looked down on me, had seen me as an equal, I would probably have given in with all sorts of "sophisticated" excuses later for my behavior.

This was a confusing time as I tread the desert of reality, going from the hot cauldron of exultant admiration to the more calming oasis of acceptance of our lives. Scott and Zelda were talented people. But the world is full of talented people. What they had that others like them didn't was luck. Scott had been lucky enough to have his talent recognized and nurtured by caring souls. Yes, he was talented. But also fortunate. Learning that was painful. It set me to thinking of other talented people I had come across, and it made me blue realizing how many were not lucky and languished. Or just learned to be content with their unremarked-on lives.

We disembarked for the Riviera, for the beautiful Villa Marie, too rich for their purses when they wanted to scrimp a bit, probably to make the writing easier for him, to relieve the pressure.

I spent many afternoons working with him on *The Great Gatsby* there, typing and retyping, loving every mutation of that story from its first *Trimalchio* roughness to its ultimate raucous gentleness. It was his greatest story, a great love story, a great American story. I still swoon when thinking of it.

And I'm so glad he let go of the Trimalchio title and its story implications. I must admit to getting that old sense of being shut out of things, the way I'd felt with that world-traveling singer in Madame Solinsky's parlor going on about organs and churches in Europe, when he explained to me its origins in the Roman *Satyricon*. Why, I thought I had been exposed to a good education with a fair smattering of Latin and Greek history, but the Trimalchio tale of a freed slave building a life of excessive luxury was one with which I wasn't familiar.

This was just after my near-surrendering to R, too, which had me sensitive about the things I didn't know, the cues that certain classes could read but were blurred to me. I felt inferior.

So, in many ways, it bothered me that he'd make Gatsby that character, a man driven by venal desires more than uplifting hopes. Did he think of me, my kind, that way—lower class without subtlety or the ability to appreciate higher things, finer ideas? It created more than one sleepless night for me pondering those possibilities. Some nights where tears dampened my pillow as I confused R with Gatsby's detractors, and I found myself in deep sympathy with Gatsby's ignorance of social mores.

But in the end, Gatsby became the gentle soul I saw in Scott himself, that called out to me. A man who himself didn't always fit in with the elites, who had to put on that suit, so to speak, with his Princeton education, his self-enlightenment, his...Zelda. Gatsby loved what glittered. So did Scott. Gatsby loved with fidelity and purpose. So did Scott. He wasn't looking down his nose at the Trimalchios of the world. He was showing the world how pure they were and how ill-treated. Scott was Trimalchio. He'd raised him up, raised all of us who strove and hoped and dreamed and yet had not the background or lineage to sip wine with the upper cliques. Scott showed the world we were good people.

This revelation calmed me. But it also led to great pain, as I saw his suntanned beauty of a wife straying, her eye taken by a young French aviator. All that came of that — even her sad attempt to end it all, by ending her existence — was just the preface for the worst to come, the complete unraveling of her mind, like fever before the sickness sets in.

After her infidelity, she became a more sympathetic character to me, maybe because her sinning lowered her, and I felt more comfortable seeing her eye to eye, so to speak. Judgment gave way to compassion on my part. Scott had his work, his glorious work. And, to some extent, I had it, too. I had something to do that gave my life importance and meaning. She had only leisure. Motherhood didn't satisfy her. And with this, I discovered I sympathized, as well. Having lost a wee one in the cradle, I'd always felt a great sense of longing for motherhood. But when little Scotty came along, a revelation occurred. I was not the baby-tending type. She was sweet as could be, an angel, a true gift from God, to be sure. But not very interesting. Changing nappies and cleaning up spills and spit-ups were no tasks for me, and I managed to always make sure the nanny or maid was called in for those chores. The Fitzgeralds understood soon enough these were duties I'd not be attending to. This, then, was a gift to me, this realization that motherhood would not have suited me. I still mourned my poor child. But I no longer mourned the loss of motherhood.

So, I understood poor Zelda's ambivalence to the role. She had the good sense not to feel guilty about it. Or act as if she cared what people thought of her lack of maternal instincts. She mostly swam and drank and partied and tried to think of outrageous things to do or say that would draw attention to her.

She thought she finally had found that something to do with her dancing back in Paris. But this just made me sadder still, watching her go off to that studio day after day, coming home sore and perspiring, wild-eyed with desperation to make a go of it. I felt like taking her aside and saying, some have it and others don't. I'd reconciled myself to that with my own small talent. Some of these talents had to be used or discarded in younger times — they didn't last. And dancing was surely one of them, requiring the nimbleness and strength of youth.

And, of course, there was that element of luck involved, as well. Even if she could have managed to shine, fortune's spotlight was focused on her husband, not on her.

I'm sure Scott didn't say much because if he did, she'd throw at him how he had his art, she had hers. No matter that her obsession made something of a mockery of his own pursuit. He was successful, after all, while she seemed to be...playing.

Nobody could say a word to her about the dancing, though, least of all lowly me, just a typist, really, for her husband's work. But I did try to talk to her more, show an interest in her, compliment her on her perseverance and dedication and suggest that it would at the very least add to her own appreciation of that fine art, and that perhaps she could do some fine writing on it to illuminate it for less-fortunate readers who didn't understand its nuances.

She looked pleased at this observation, but it didn't sway her from her routine. Routine is a powerful thing, giving meaning to life even when there's no meaning in the routine.

By the time her mind broke completely, I was in sympathy with her, wishing Scott would have been more forceful with her about letting the dancing go, seeing it as the trigger for the blow to her sanity. You can't watch someone heading for a cliff without feeling a powerful urge to help hold them back. That's how I felt, sick at heart watching her lunge forward. And I anguished over how much to say, whether being critical was cruel or kind.

I would go visit her in that sanitarium in Europe where she first landed, and then at Hopkins when we all flitted back to home country, shaken and tired and irritated with life itself. I had to do it on the sly because he was awful protective of her and didn't like just anybody going to see her anytime. When he heard I was seeing her almost every day back in the States, he put the lid on it, saying he needed me to be typing his manuscripts. I'd show up, he'd be hung over, and I'd be typing up her stuff instead, although he didn't know it. Then I'd leave early and go see her.

She was like an angel then, so soft and quiet and wounded, really. She'd say to me, "Bea, why does Scott think my life doesn't belong to me?" And what could I say? I didn't know. I'd just shrug and tell her she had to get better for his sake as well as hers.

Truth be told, I wondered when one married whose life belonged to whom? With Jeremy and me, I have no doubt I would have lived in his fine, strong shadow all my life, quite happily, too. And I knew many couples who seemed hard to tell apart anymore. Zelda was no different, part of a whole, no longer her own. It was something I pondered and fretted on, awed by the mystery of coupling that produced this separate entity entirely, appalled by how one's individuality could be consumed by it. Marriage involved sacrifice.

And that was the God's honest truth. He was sacrificing himself to be sure. He was sinking and sinking, the liquor a poison to his life. Even the doctors told him it was no good how he was drinking. No good for him, no good for her. But he'd protest, tell them that the liquor more or less was his muse. His muse! No, his Morpheus, pushing him into a sleep while the world marched by.

He went out of date. Like last year's styles, last season's music. He couldn't face that. It was all he had — the constancy of youth through his writing. And with his public looking the other way, he couldn't avoid looking in the mirror himself and seeing that it was all going, just as it does with the rest of us, the smooth skin showing fine wrinkles, the bright hair dulling, the shine in the eye clouding. Why couldn't he see he was just hastening that journey with his drinking?

I tried watering down the gin once or twice. He just drank more. And had me type a page of manuscript in which a character says the cruelest things of his secretary — I will not repeat them, they made me weep — of whom he suspects "pilfery, stealing gin thinking that would help her steal all the things her employer could not give her if he wanted to: how to be pretty, intelligent, witty and loved, none of which had ever been hers nor would likely come into her life now that she was thick of waist and dull in the head. She just wasn't born to be part of the good set." Well, you see, I have repeated some of them. And even now I do shudder deep in my heart to read such mean things. I'd never pretended to be a Zelda or even in the same class as him and her. But I do think I'm handsome if not beautiful with some modicum of intelligence. And I do think I have things to say that might be of meaning to some folks. I'd hoped so, at least...

CHAPTER FOURTEEN

ON AND ON she wrote, even beyond dinnertime and late into the night... until she couldn't write anymore. She'd not finished, but the next day, she managed to bang out a synopsis of the rest of the story.

She did a quick read-through and emailed it off to Malcolm with a note: "Best I can do for now. Hope you can do something with it. Let's call it *The Last Romantics.*"

And then she fell into sleep again, a dreamless void, awakening late the next morning, hoping to see something back from Malcolm. But the day passed with no word, and she packed up her things, sat in the garden, had a quiet dinner with Becky and Bob, called Jim to give him her travel details, and the next morning....one last, long chattering hour with her sister, as Becky drove her into Baltimore to catch the train.

After a weary journey through green back to brown, as she whispered her farewells to the shy delicate willows starting to unfold along the train route, as she recoiled from the window seeing some ice and snow patches still on banks of the Hudson, she arrived in Vermont at eight that evening. Jim was there with a bouquet of flowers, and she nearly cried when he embraced her, so happy was she to be in the arms of someone who loved her without question, conditions, or judgment.

෴

The next day, she prickled with nervous energy again waiting to hear back from Malcolm. He'd said he'd wanted something from her by Monday, so she'd figured he'd look at it right away. Maybe that had been a mistake, she thought as the afternoon wore on. Agents always said they'd look at things quickly and then would get back to you in six weeks or more.

While she obsessively checked email and made perfunctory stabs at writing more of *Wishful Thinking* revisions, Jim tinkered somewhere in the house. She heard him on the phone at one point, and she waited crossly for him to get off, wondering if Malcolm would try to call her on the landline. But Jim was good about taking any interruption calls — they had Call Waiting — especially when it came to her writing.

Jim avoided her most of the day, and she was grateful for it. She knew he was giving her space to write, to work on her writing business. She also suspected he was staying out of her hair so that he'd not have to answer any questions about his job-hunting, which, as far as she could see, was nonexistent. She hadn't realized until she was home that she'd secretly hoped he would volunteer a report, tell her with quiet enthusiasm that he'd applied to this place in Maryland or that business outside of Baltimore. She brooded about this, about having another confrontation with him, throwing an ultimatum his way. What would it be — get a job or I leave again? Maybe he'd get used to the leaving. Why couldn't this problem solve itself on its own?

By five, she finally let herself truly believe Malcolm wouldn't be getting back to her that day. She closed up shop—for her that meant leaving the office on the back of the house and being a normal wife.

Rounding the corner, she was surprised to hear music playing. "Baker Street" was wafting into the hall again.

One more year and he'd be happy...

But Jim certainly looked happy right now. Two champagne flutes sat on their coffee table. When she looked confused, he just lifted his eyebrows mysteriously, went to the kitchen and fetched the bottle of chilled bubbly.

"What's this for?" she asked as he uncorked the bottle and poured them each a glass. She took a preemptive sip, eager to feel the kick. She thought, for one joyous moment, he'd landed a job.

"A celebration," he said. "A sale. I sold my paintings."

She nearly spat out her drink. As it was, bubbles burned her nose.

"To whom? I mean, that's great! But who—"

"Some dude in California. Sold them on eBay."

She smiled, despite her disappointment, thinking then that he'd tell her they'd gone for fifty bucks or less, covering the cost of materials at least. That would be a relief. And maybe an end to this silly exercise. But when he revealed the price, she was shocked. It was nearly twice her last advance.

"You're kidding."

"Nope. Was on the phone with him earlier. Worked out the deal—am getting an electronic down payment, already in the bank. The rest will come when I deliver the first three paintings. Final payment after the last two are received."

Stunned, she collapsed on to the sofa. "But, Jim…you're not an artist. I mean, does he know you're not an artist?"

Jim was nonplussed by her implied insult. He was too giddy to notice. "Who's to say who's an artist? I'm an artist to this guy. He collects new painters, says he spots trends, buys before they become big. I looked him up. He's legit. Has made a ton. I probably could have waited for more money, but…bird in the hand, you know." He looked down, a little sheepish now.

"Jim…." She couldn't process it. Her mind was simultaneously numb and moving at light speed. She felt…low. They'd just perpetrated a fraud, really. Jim was no artist, regardless what he said, and he had to know it. He'd only dabbled in it to prove a point, not to really express anything. But deep down, there was something even more troubling. If Jim could make so much money on his garbage through plain, dumb luck, what were the chances she'd find real appreciation and financial reward for her real artistic efforts? If drek found an appreciative audience, what did it matter if that same cultural audience liked her? It was as if Jim were proving to her that her quest was fruitless, that her audience had no taste.

"Imagination without skill," she murmured at last, a Tom Stoppard quote she'd used often to describe modern art they didn't like.

"But imagination is what's selling, honey." He sat next to her, held her hand. "I look at it this way. It's like those big chefs on those chef contest shows you like to watch. They taste so much good stuff that their palate kinda gets ruined for more good stuff. So it's only the way-out stuff that really excites them anymore. If you're just producing good stuff, it's not gonna grab them. You just have to hit on the one way-out thing that gets them running in your direction."

"Like a herd, you mean?"

"Yeah. Guess so."

She pulled away. "You feel absolutely no shame?"

He shook his head. "None." Now his voice and face changed, brows coming together in annoyance or hurt, she couldn't tell.

"But, Jim, you didn't...I mean, what is it you were expressing in those paintings anyway? What did you tell him? What did you write up on eBay describing them?"

He held up a finger and disappeared, returning in a few seconds with some papers, the printouts of his eBay offering and email correspondence.

She could barely read through them through her irritation-blurred eyes, but it was all, as Jim had said, "legit." He'd not pretended to be something he wasn't. "Self-taught painter," he'd described himself to the guy. "Jim Lazlo" — a pang of envy coursed through her at that as she mourned not using her own name on her writing. And the name of the collection was "Sky Blue Fantasy."

She couldn't help it — she laughed at that.

"That's the name of the wall paint you used," she said, pointing to the title.

"Yup."

The description of the pieces was similarly straightforward: six panels depicting artist's interpretation of Sky Blue Fantasy, blending shapes and shades common to suburban America into a pleasing panorama.

She'd read similar descriptions at art exhibits.

"Were you consciously mocking the art world?"

"Nope. Just being honest. I like that color. Sky Blue Fantasy." He sat back, refilled his flute and swigged more champagne. "You should be happy. I made some money. I found a job. Something I enjoyed, too."

She sat up straight, as if touched by an electric wire. Oh, no. "This is not a job," she said, tapping the papers.

"It could be. If this fellow's sale gets me known. It could lead to others. Could lead to regular gigs."

"Painting canvases with Sherwin-Williams wall paint?" She sank back into the sofa, hardly able to think. "First of all, it's unsteady. Second of all, it's not real!" She stood and paced to the window, hugging herself. "It makes fun of art. It's not real art! And what we need — what I need — is a regular paycheck so I can take the time to produce real art, not this sham crap that makes fun of me." She heard her voice tremble, and fought back sudden tears. Why was Jim so dense about this?

"Makes fun of you?" Jim got up and came to her, but she moved away when he tried to hug her. "You're taking this way too personally." Then his tone hardened. "I thought you'd be happy – if not for me, then for our income stream. I thought this was what you wanted. This is a lot of expenses covered at the very least. More than what you've brought in last year. This, along with your most recent advance, can go a long way."

She sighed, but she wouldn't cry. She was past that. It wasn't what she wanted, but what was that anyway? She wanted Malcolm to contact her. Wanted him to say, hey, I not only loved your work-up, I actually talked to an editor about it already and sold it. Contract's in the mail.

Instead, her husband had managed to make a goodly sum by selling fakery.

"I have a headache," she whispered. "I need to lie down."

She wanted, most of all, to go home.

The morning seemed to wipe everything away except the dull ache of disappointment. Jim was subdued. She could tell he was angry with her. After all, he thought he'd solved a money problem. But maybe it wasn't a money problem. Maybe it was a...commitment problem. She didn't want to live hand-to-mouth. She wanted to feel secure. And she wanted to know that he loved her enough to give her that security and that he believed in her talent enough to give her the time and space to work on her...*art*.

She checked her email while waiting for coffee to brew. A few fun notes from Jackie and Marie, a little about writing and the book business but mostly about their family lives. Jackie had three children, Marie none. They had the usual sets of problems for people their age — parents who needed care, bills that needed paying, plans that needed making. As she got ready to respond to one of them, a new email came in. And here at last was something that made her heart pound with excitement. A note from Malcolm.

I'll be out most of the day but hope to read this by tomorrow at the latest.

That was it? He'd told her to hurry, and now he was going to be ...out? This was precisely why she hated the idea of having an agent. He wasn't helping her progress. He was holding her back.

Holding you back from what, she asked herself. What would you do with this opus if left to your own devices?

She shook off her irritation as best she could. She had to make progress on *Wishful Thinking*. At least that was real. More real than that bogus art Jim had just sold. Jim! There was an authenticity to genre writing. It didn't pretend to be something it wasn't. At its best, it was just good storytelling. Damn good storytelling in the right hands. And she'd try to make hers as good as it got.

Everything disappeared as she typed — Beatrice's story, the Fitzgeralds, Jim, her worries. Even her memories didn't tease her as she worked. She was determined to make great progress on Jake and Belinda's story, to take them beyond the "bears in the boat" to the "black moment" and into the HEA. She settled in.

CHAPTER FIFTEEN

WISHFUL THINKING – CHAPTER NINETEEN
Belinda might be angry with him, but he'd rather have her mad than dead. He'd thought about it for hours — back in Baltimore after he'd driven her there, on the drive to New Jersey when she insisted on going back to work a few days later, while working at his laptop in her apartment. Yes, in her apartment. They were a commuting couple. Commuting for sex. Sometimes to his place, now at hers.

The morning papers were filled with a story about an "eco-terrorist," a man writing scathing letters to the mayor and the paper itself. He was the main suspect now, but Jake didn't buy it. The eco-terrorist angle was a red herring. The world was full of people with imagination without skill, he thought irritably. They all grabbed on to the latest new theory without thinking it through. All right. He'd take matters into his own hands. He set up a meeting with a private detective.

Private Investigator Sean Castleton, a stocky man with very short brown hair and a bristly mustache to match, had quickly responded to his call and gone over the case. And he'd agreed that Belinda might indeed be the target of some violent predator, not the mayor, Payton Barstow, for whom she worked. Castleton wouldn't rule Barstow out as the ultimate focus of this madman, though. So that meant he'd be digging into Barstow's life a bit—something that made Jake nervous. What if he found out things that could affect Belinda's job? All pols had skeletons of some kind in their closets. Better angry than dead, he reminded himself.

Castleton had also nodded his head to Jake's theory that the "Avenging Gunman"—the anonymous note-writer upset about development—was likely a dead end.

"What self-respecting eco-terrorist would drive an SUV – or even know where to borrow one?" he'd asked in his no-nonsense Jersey accent. He'd look into it, but he didn't think they'd find the real motive there.

"What is the motive?" Jake had asked.

"The usual – money, revenge, passion. I'll check all of them." Sean had flipped his notebook closed and stuffed it into his pocket.

Look into them all—including Belinda's past boyfriends, her ex-fiance. What if she found out? She'd not specifically told him not to hire a detective when he'd suggested it. She'd said she'd think about it.

After they left the restaurant, Jake felt even more uneasy. He wasn't usually so impulsive about action, but her jeopardy required it. He couldn't risk losing the woman he loved to a sniper's bullet.

The woman he loved.

As he walked to his car, he let the thought sink in. Loved. He'd not felt this way since…. Well, he'd never felt this way. His youth had been consumed with responsibility after his parents' tragic deaths. At the age of eighteen, he'd taken on everything just so he and his brother could stay in their family home, so that Chris's life could be stable. He'd had help—neighbors, some relatives from England who'd come for extended stays, but he'd quickly learned everything he needed to know---from balancing a checkbook to making dinner to doing laundry—and had hired help for those things he didn't have time or inclination for. He'd rarely thought of what he wanted out of life. He'd done college in three years, started work right after, and bought his own company within five years using investments his parents had made.

He'd made love to women, but never really loved. Not like this. Not the kind of love that made him feel complete. If Belinda were to leave, or something were to happen to her, he'd be an emotional amputee, missing a critical part of the whole. He'd be just Jake again. Not Jake-and-Belinda. How quickly he'd turned in to a different person, a blending of the two of them.

God, it was both wonderful and horrible to feel this way. Wonderful to feel so alive and connected to the universe. Horrible to know that this could lead to heartbreak or disaster if he let it consume them.

The Jersey air was tinged with a metallic odor, the smell of making what the world was taking, to paraphrase the Trenton sign. The sun beamed heat on his shoulders while the breeze was cool.

If Belinda found out he'd hired a detective, if the detective unearthed something she or her boss didn't want seen, it might be over.

Well, that's part of love, I suppose, he mused. *Being willing to sacrifice it for the one you care about.*

When she returned that evening, he was jumpy and cross. He'd been too distracted to work, and he had a pile of action items requiring his attention. He'd have to go back home soon. But he'd found himself constantly scrolling through websites and doing background reading on the modus operandi of cases such as these. Adding to his unease – he'd been unable to connect with Belinda late in the day. Her office phone kept going to voice mail, and the one time he tried the cell, she'd snapped she was in a meeting.

Finally, at nearly nine, the door opened, and she appeared, tired and looking frazzled.

"Let me take you out," he said, kissing her lightly on the cheek. "Or whip up something here. Don't forget – I'm not a bad cook."

She gave him a halfhearted smile. "You're wonderful in the kitchen. And elsewhere. But I'm not that hungry. Had something late in the day."

He studied her. "Something's bothering you. I'm sorry about the interruption. I couldn't reach you on your office line...."

She shook her head, not looking at him. "That's all right. My office line...it went...kerfluey."

He straightened. "What precisely happened?"

Avoiding his gaze, she struggled out of her shoes. "The line was...broken," she said.

"Broken?"

Now she stood upright and looked at him. "I think the cleaning lady must have run over it with her vacuum."

He inhaled sharply. "It was torn out of the wall?"

"No, the line was kind of...torn apart."

"Ripped? Or were the ends cleanly cut?" He ran his fingers through his hair. This was maddening. If she couldn't see she was a target—thank God he'd hired Castleton.

"What is this—the third degree?"

He gripped her by both arms and stared into her eyes. "It was cut, wasn't it? Someone deliberately cut your phone line, Belinda. Why—who knew you'd be staying late tonight? Tell me what happened, everything, who you talked to, who you saw, what you did—"

She shook free of his grasp, and he saw tears coming to her eyes.

"It was a normal workday, okay? Crazy busy. Payton all over me for some stupid mistake on a flyer that an intern made, but I should have proofed it. Payton trying to write one of his own speeches—always a mistake. And I'm already creeped out, so don't add to it!"

She walked into the living room and slumped in a chair. He followed but stood to the side, his arms crossed, while he inwardly seethed. Why wouldn't she let him help her?

"Why were you 'creeped out'?" he asked as softly as he could manage.

"You know. Empty office. Everything going on. I was jumping at my own shadow." She sat, her hands between her legs, hunched over. She was bothered, but she didn't want to worry him. Okay, he'd work with that. He sat down next to her and put his arm around her. When she leaned against his shoulder, he breathed a slow sigh of relief.

"No one else around except you and Payton?" he prodded.

"Not that I could tell," she said on a breath. "But I thought I heard someone in the stairwell...it was nothing, though. And there's a security guard at the door, you know."

He closed his eyes as he imagined her fear. Then he realized—she'd taken the stairs, not the elevator. She'd been too afraid to use it. At least she was aware. But it cut him to think of her so frightened.

"Belinda," he began carefully, after kissing the top of her head and stroking her shoulder, "please, come home with me." Home. His home.

She paused, and he felt victory near. Then she said, "I can't. Too much to do. A big parade coming up. Payton will be in it. Founder's Day thing. All hands on deck."

A parade? She'd be in the public eye.

As if reading his mind, she said, "Security will be crawling all over. Plain clothes guys and gals, too. They'll probably make up half the crowd."

He was about to protest, but she silenced that thought and roused others by trailing her finger down his chest, rubbing him softly, then with more pressure as she leaned up for an intimate kiss.

"I don't want to talk about this anymore," she whispered, turning and pressing into him. He felt her breasts crush against his chest, her hot breath on his neck, the scent of her juniper perfume. "I don't want to talk at all." She straddled him and began unbuttoning his shirt, tugging it down so that eventually its sleeves pinned his arms close to his body.

"What do you want?" he managed to say, huskily.

"You. As my slave." She quickly whipped her silky top over her head. "Take off my bra. With your teeth." She smiled and leaned in, and he forgot everything they'd just said.

CHAPTER SIXTEEN

BELINDA AND JAKE would have to wait. She had more crises for them to face, but she couldn't do it now. Too tired.

Absolutely bushed, her shoulders and back aching, and her wrists smarting, too, Kate stood after pounding away for five hours straight on their tale, mulling the bears yet to throw in that boat. She thought she had them all lined up in her head, and it was just a matter of getting them into the darn dinghy in the right order at just the right moment. If her editor wanted more tension, she'd give it to her. She preferred writing the suspenseful parts, in fact, rather than the steamy scenes. She'd noticed that Alice didn't bug her so much for the sex if she included enough tension.

Kate was a combination "pantser" and "plotter" author. She didn't entirely do the "seat of her pants" kind of writing that some authors felt comfortable with. She had to have a rough idea of where her characters were headed. She didn't plot obsessively — she knew Jackie sometimes made elaborate color-coded charts for all her characters and story events — but she did jot down bullet points and sometimes jumped ahead to write a climactic scene just so it would stop nagging at her as she worked through the Dreaded Middle.

"Jim!" she called out, wondering if she could convince him to fix dinner or be up for Chinese takeout. They should be more frugal with their food budget, but meal-planning always went by the wayside when she was deep in the midst of deadlines. Maybe she needed to talk more to Jim about that responsibility, making it clear that she wanted him to be proactive with that task. Maybe that would help her feel better about him not working...or working at his "art."

Then she remembered the last big meal he'd cooked for them—a tough chicken, burned rice, salad with pieces of lettuce the size of book pages. No, scratch that idea.

"Jim!" she called again. Music continued from the basement. She'd mentally blocked it out while deep in Jake and Belinda's story. Something old—the Doobie Brothers' "What a fool believes."

> *"What seems to be*
> *Is always better than nothing...."*

He probably didn't hear her. With a sigh, trying to tamp down irritation so they could have a nice evening together—she so wanted to just relax and be happy—she headed for the basement, opening the door while deliberately taking calming breaths.

"Jim," she said sweetly, as she walked down the stairs. "I was thinking we could go out to—"

Calming breath left her as she stopped breathing altogether. Jim was sprawled on the floor next to his canvas, paint spilled on the floor—Sky Blue Fantasy on his hand and shirt, spattered on his still face. Her world stopped, her eyes widened, as one word came to mind: *No!*

"Jim! Jim!" She ran to him, shaking him, forgetting every scrap of first aid information she'd ever heard or seen. She started to sob, angry at him, sorry for him, sorry for herself, worried, consumed with a range of emotions as if overdosing on a drug, reaching instinctively for her cell phone buried in her jeans pocket. "Jim, wake up," she cried as she punched in 911 with shaking fingers.

As the operator came on the line, Jim roused, his eyes blinking, his mouth forming a soft "What?"

Kate managed to gulp out that her husband had collapsed and gave the woman their address, even as Jim reached for her arm and shook his head.

"I'm fine," he mumbled, rubbing the back of his head now. "Jus' took nap."

"You're not fine," she said, suddenly angry at him. He couldn't be not fine! Being not fine wasn't fair. "What happened?"

He tried to sit up, and she tried to keep him down. She gave in to his stubbornness and helped him sit, at which point he grimaced and reached for his right knee, rubbing it.

"Okay, I remember," he murmured, shaking his head again as if irritated with himself. "I turned, caught my foot on the tarp—" he pointed to the plastic sheeting on which he'd spread his supplies "—and... I must have conked my head when I fell."

"How long have you been out?" she asked, now awash with guilt for not checking on him earlier. She and her stories, her silly Jake and Belinda stories.

He smiled at her. "Felt like a few seconds to me. Have no idea."

Soon the doorbell was ringing, EMTs were heading downstairs, neighbors stopped by—activity swamped her and Jim as they were enveloped in a blanket of caring.

The EMTs thought Jim might have a concussion and had at least twisted something in his knee. They loaded him into the ambulance for transport to the hospital. Kate's neighbor Keith, a lifelong Vermonter, worked it out so his wife, Pat, would drive Kate's car there, in case she needed it to bring Jim home later. Grateful for the plan and the optimistic thought, she handed over her car keys and jumped into the ambulance to accompany Jim.

"Mrs. Lazlo?" A young doctor strode into their curtained cubicle in the ER, hand extended.

She shook it as he introduced himself as Dr. Wilkins and proceeded to give them the good news that Jim didn't have any broken bones, just a muscle strain in his leg that would be helped by a cortisone shot and ace bandage along with a little physical therapy. He'd most likely passed out as much from the paint fumes as anything else—he'd admitted to keeping the window closed because of the cold, at which they'd exchanged knowing looks. Even Jim had found the Vermont spring too cold? That was rich, something they'd laugh about later.

"So, I'm going to discharge you. Just call this number to schedule a follow-up appointment," he said, handing them some papers.

Of course, it took another two hours before they were ready to leave. Tons of papers to sign, the shot to be administered, a short wait to make sure he wasn't allergic to the meds, and finally…as the moon hung in a midnight sky…she pushed him in a wheelchair to the parking lot, easily finding her car where Keith had told her it would be. He and his wife had offered to stay with her, but she'd shooed them home earlier, grateful they'd thought to handle the transportation when it had been the furthest thing from her mind.

Home within twenty minutes, she helped Jim hobble up to bed, the tension of the day now releasing as she was able to channel her energy into pampering him. She put a pillow under his affected leg, and brought him a sandwich and tea on a tray. She herself hadn't eaten a thing, but she was too keyed up to think of fixing herself something.

"I'm pretty sleepy," he said, almost in apology as he left half the sandwich uneaten.

"I think they gave you some pain meds that might do that," she said. "I can go check the papers…."

He grabbed her hand. "That's all right. I'm just going to snooze. You okay?"

It was just like Jim to ask about her. She saw the worry in his eyes and wanted to wipe it away, but he'd know if she was faking.

"No," she said in a small voice. "Yes. Maybe. I'm just relieved. Don't go doing that again, okay?" She was surprised to hear her voice shaking.

"Yeah, we can't afford it."

She punched him in the arm. "That's not what I meant. We have insurance."

"You coming to bed?"

"In a few. I'm pretty juiced right now." She might not have eaten, but she'd accepted a cup of coffee from a nurse's aide while at the ER. "Let me know if you need anything. I'll be up soon."

She took his tray away, tucked him in like a child, and kissed him gently on the cheek.

"Thanks," he murmured before closing his eyes. And she stared at him, wanting to imprint the image on her heart like a tattoo. Jim-and-Kate. Not just Jim. God, how she loved him! That's what made it so hard. She still loved him.

She went to the basement after putting away the dishes, and she cleaned up his mess, mopping up the spilled paint with rags she placed outside in a bin and gently removing his work-in-progress to a safe distance from any of the still-tacky spills. Now, the paintings made her smile, thinking of Jim and his lack of guile or irony, his straightforward, childlike enjoyment.

"Oh, Jim," she whispered. She felt shaken. The evening's events caught up with her, and her whole body trembled. She had to place her fist in her mouth to keep her sobs silent. "Oh, Jim."

Years ago, the Litany of Events had led them here. Or rather, had led Jim to lead her here, and she'd felt rescued by his strong decision-making, his will.

The sale of her first book had been quickly followed by fear and heartache. The informational interview in New York that Jim had been off to—it was to take place on September 11, 2001. He'd called her that morning, though, to tell her the disappointing news that the interview was being canceled, or at least postponed, since he'd had a call from his contact saying something had come up.

Kate had felt disappointed and irritated. She could sense that Jim wasn't too upset about the change in plans, and that had tipped her off to the fact that maybe Jim wasn't as passionate about a career move as she'd thought. She'd wanted to shake him, to tell him he had to choose something, some path. And she'd encouraged him to at least stop in a distant cousin's office, a financier, to say hello. Jim had promised to do so.

The cousin's office had been in the World Trade Center.

For hours after the crisis, Kate had wept and worried and been near collapse. Phone lines were tied up, and she couldn't reach Jim. She'd been convinced he was dead, and it was her fault. She'd nagged him into going to that building. She didn't know how she'd face his parents. She didn't know how she'd face herself.

At last, late afternoon, he'd gotten through to her. He'd not gone to see his cousin, after making a phone call and finding out he wasn't in that day. Both of them had been spared! She'd cried so hard with relief, she couldn't speak. She'd promised herself to be a better wife, a better person.

But that resolution was easy. Living it was hard. She became consumed by worry, beset by panic attacks. When Jim returned from New York, they set about living to the fullest. She became pregnant. But she miscarried. They tried again. With the same result.

Then her mother passed away, and Jim's brother entered the Marines, and there was a whole new set of worries as he deployed. When he came back unhurt, Kate thought for sure she'd lose the sense of doom that always dogged her. But it just wouldn't let go.

And finally, Jim had said, "Let's go visit my grandfather in Vermont, get away from all this." All this — what he'd really meant was the world of fear and doubt she'd built for herself and, by extension, him. He'd done some part-time work here and there, temp jobs, some bookkeeping, during those years, but mostly his main job had been looking after his basket-case wife.

For the first time in her life, she developed asthma. She'd ended up in the hospital several times when asthma attacks reduced her to a wheezing, panicky ball of fear.

And just as she'd stood by Jim's side in the ER this night, he'd stood by hers, holding her hand, nodding at the doctor's reassurances. Now she understood how hard that was, being the healthy one while your beloved suffers.

"Oh, Jim," she whispered again.

The world was a cruel place, and she didn't want to face it alone.

After turning out the basement light, she went to her office. She sat silently in her chair for a long time, letting her breath and heart rate return to normal. She blew her nose, pushed her hair out of her face, and began tapping away on *Wishful Thinking*.

CHAPTER SEVENTEEN

WISHFUL THINING – CHAPTER TWENTY-FOUR
God, how he loved her. That's what made this all so damn hard.

All hell was breaking loose. Belinda had fallen into his arms when he'd picked her up at the train station, beating him on the chest, so angry she could barely speak. His detective had turned up something—about Payton and his infidelities. The resulting bad press had caught her off guard, and he knew, even though she didn't say it, that it had caused a certain amount of heartache, too, as she wrestled with losing respect for a man she'd admired. But the capper was the fact that some enterprising reporter had identified the source of the story as a "private detective investigating the recent attacks." She'd put two and two together and figured out who might have hired the PI that had unleashed this nightmare on her professional life.

Jake suspected, in fact, that Belinda's trip to see him was prompted by this anger at him, and that she might have been planning a breakup, or at least a cooling off. The only thing that had stopped her from completely running away from him, though, was the other bit of hell that had crashed in on her. She'd had another close call on the way to Baltimore. A man had tried to push her into the path of the arriving train at the New Jersey station. She'd lost her phone in the process, but she'd managed to keep her footing — and her life.

Now she was in his bed again. The heat of the moment had turned in to another kind of heat. She lay sleeping in the crook of his arm while he stared at the ceiling, pondering the future, both immediate and long-term.

He wanted her to stay with him. He could protect her. He wanted to take her away while the police and Sean Castleton did their jobs. He wanted...this. Forever. The world was a cruel place, and he wanted her to know she didn't need to face it alone.

"Mmm," she murmured, rousing in the blue light of dawn, her eyes fluttering open to see him. She smiled. Then, as though memories of the previous day and evening were coming back, she frowned and sat bolt upright.

"I should go," she said, shaking her head. That beautiful tousled head. That cherubic face. Those sparkling eyes.

Before she could slide out of bed, he grabbed her arm. "Please, stay," he said softly.

"We've been over this," she said. "You can't run my life."

"I don't want to run it. I want to save it."

"That's just it. I'm still not convinced I'm the target!" She turned to him, letting the sheet drop, revealing her exquisite breasts. How did she expect him to argue now?

"You were pushed," he said. "You said so yourself. You felt like the target!"

"I was influenced by the hyper-panicky atmosphere after a really shitty day," she said. "Thanks to you and that Sam Spade you hired."

He sat up, leaning against the headboard. "Mr. Spade will get a piece of my mind and a termination notice. His clumsiness doesn't change the fact that you were in danger. It's you this madman is after."

"Now that we know Payton is diddling the Barbie doll in the office and that said Barbie has ties to a developer he's been standing in the way of, I'd say it's a good bet Payton's the target!" She yanked at the sheet to cover herself.

He sat up to put his hand on her shoulder. "But, why, Belinda? Why try to knock off someone when your goal is to get a project okayed? I mean, the money isn't worth the penalty the developer would have to pay in jail should he be caught. There are easier ways to get rid of a Payton Barstow. Like giving tons to his opponent in the next election."

"People get crazy in politics," she said. "You have no idea. But you're missing the point. The point is that you—" she jabbed him in the chest "—shouldn't be interfering in my life like that. It's...demeaning. As if I'm a child."

He winced. He still felt the age difference acutely. He suspected she'd intended the accusation to hit just that bull's-eye.

"I can't help it," he said. "I love you." They'd not uttered the words to each other, and he realized they'd both been avoiding it, both been trying to delude themselves into thinking this relationship was one long one-night stand, one long tango with no further meaning. He watched her face. Her lips parted, and he knew her affirming response sat on an unarticulated breath, that his actions, trying to "save" her, had put a hold on what she felt. She closed her mouth, bit her lip, looked down, swallowed.

"I'm sorry. That's obviously putting another pressure on you."

She whipped up to look at him. "No. I'm the one who's sorry. I know how you feel. I know because I feel it, too." She clasped her hands in her lap and stared at them, not him, now. "I love you, too."

Despite himself, he chuckled. "It is a burden if you confess it like that."

She smiled and shook her head. "We're a pair. How did we get here?"

"I think a more apt question is, where do we go from here?"

She turned to him. "You mentioned getting away. How about that? We get away for a few days. I think that's about all the planning I have in me right now." When he brightened and reached for her to embrace, she held up an index finger. "On one condition."

"Name it, and the world is yours."

"Fire Mr. Spade."

"Done."

He grasped her finger and kissed it, pulling it into his mouth. Then she fell into him, splaying her hand across his chest. "We're hopeless," she whispered as she leaned up to kiss his neck.

"No, I'd say we're filled with hope." At least, he wanted her to be. He knew he was. He lost himself in the moment, the throbbing, moaning ecstasy of loving each other, and every time he whispered what he wanted to do, she responded with an enthusiastic yes in words and actions. He nudged her legs apart and…

CHAPTER EIGHTEEN

IT TOOK HIM more than a week, but Malcolm finally got back to Kate. By then, she knew why he'd been delayed. Publishers Marketplace had carried the story of his selling, at auction, a big new literary novel by some phenom from the South. It made her angry and envious, neither emotions she wanted to feel, so then she felt guilty on top of that. She shouldn't begrudge someone else success, nor Malcolm's attention to that deal.

When he finally responded about her proposal, it was with an odd combination of encouragement and dampening of expectations.

"This is good," he wrote in his email, "really good. Let me see what I can do."

She'd immediately fired off a thank-you email, asking him if he needed more. What she really wanted to know was what the "see what I can do" meant. Was he going to show it to editors or get back to her with suggestions for revisions? She should have just asked outright, she realized after she'd sent the danged note. Why did she try to hide what she really wanted?

Meanwhile, she checked their bank accounts online, and, darned if the first payment for Jim's artwork wasn't there in checking. He was right. The "dude" was legit. She'd asked for his name and Googled him. Everything Jim had said about him was true. He was wealthy — trust fund, not hard work — and looked for "emerging artists who might be ignored by more mainstream outlets due to circumstance and background." He knew that sometimes he'd end up with "junk," but it was always "junk he enjoyed." He wasn't stupid. He didn't pay top dollar for his finds. But Jim's pieces had been part of a series, so he'd gotten a good sum for the bunch of them combined.

That consoled her. At least he had his eyes open. He wasn't leaping to the conclusion that Jim truly was an artist. He was buying what he liked, and if it turned into something valuable, all the better.

She wrote Marie, then Jackie, while she worked on *Wishful Thinking.* As she pounded out the story, she kept a glance on her email to see if they would respond. Marie did with the usual sympathy for the endless waits in publishing, and then her own tale of woe.

So, you know Jenny Deerborn, that gal we met at RWA? She finally got published, a gorgeous women's fiction/literary fiction thing. I read it – we were critique partners. I think I told you when she sold. Her book's out now, and she went to her local bookstore to find it. Two copies. Shelved in general fiction. Spine out. No co-op deal. She said she'd rather they just burn it. Nobody'll find her in general fiction – nobody would know to look for her – and at least a book-burning would get her some publicity.

She did remember Jenny, a sweet gal. Marie had told her about her sale, and they'd been sure her book would get a lot of buzz. But if her publisher wasn't plunking down the cash to get her on the new-releases table or end caps—the co-op deals—she was right. Having the book burned would get her better attention.

Maybe we can get somebody to rail against it from a pulpit, Kate wrote back.

Naw, nothing salacious in it, I'm afraid. If anything, the churchgoers would like it. It has a nice faith element in it. In fact, Booklist assigned it to an inspirational reviewer. It's not an inspirational. And the review – ahem – reflected that.

Kate cringed. There but for the grace of God....

While she had to admit her green-eyed monster had surfaced a bit at this deal announcement a year ago, she'd been able to put that envy to rest and had honestly thought, based on Marie's opinion of the story, that this book would go far. But publishers put the majority of their marketing dollars in promoting books to booksellers, not to actual readers, and in Jenny's case, it sounded as if they'd not even done that. Nothing was put on a "new releases" table because the store manager thought it was a good read. Publishers paid for that in-store real estate.

Now, all the promotion would fall on Jenny, and Kate suspected the gal didn't have big bucks to spend on her own advertising and book tours. She was defeated right out of the gate, unless her book happened to catch a bit of good luck. Her sales would probably clock in below the fifty percent of the print run mark, especially if the print run was overly optimistic. And her Bookscan numbers would brand her the rest of her writing life. Poor gal. She might have to write under a pseudonym to get published again. And, according to Marie, she'd written a damn fine book.

It amazes me that publishers do not know how to sell books to readers, Kate wrote. *They know how to buy the books from authors. How to edit the books. How to provide the cover art. They do not know how to actually sell the books.*

Amazon knows how, Marie countered.

And they loathe Amazon, Kate wrote.

She and Marie shared an agnosticism about Amazon that Jackie didn't. Jackie had bought into the anti-Amazon sentiment of many authors and big publishing companies, seeing them as a corporate Godzilla killing artists. Kate and Marie tended to think that big corporate publishers did the same things, but in a more genteel way, and, in fact, Amazon did actually know how to sell books to real readers, so what was the problem? Big publishers were the old blood, Amazon the new. And like most old money, the publishing houses looked down their noses on outré arrivistes.

Big publishing houses liked to think they weren't selling something so much as offering...art. Their accountants and finance people knew better, even if the editorial side didn't. The book business was part of the entertainment industry. And while other parts of that industry, from music to movies to TV and beyond, had figured out long ago how to market directly to their consumers, the publishing business stayed stuck in some nineteenth and twentieth century model, occasionally muttering about the decline in readership like a spinster complaining of morals today, prim pinky finger raised by her teacup.

Kate often wondered, in fact, if readership was declining because of the dearth of good products out there. Had publishing houses created wary consumers by offering too many books that simply weren't good reads? Why should a reader plunk down twenty bucks for a so-so book when she could rent a few movies for the same amount and have a more satisfying experience? It was all so subjective, and she fought being too judgmental, often losing the battle.

It was about making a buck, and Marie had confided to Kate she was thinking of jumping on to the self-publishing bandwagon, which Amazon had made so easy for authors. She was held back mostly by peer pressure. Every writing group she belonged to had a strong anti-Amazon contingent, mostly made up of authors who'd done well in traditional publishing and, to Marie, didn't seem to like the idea that maybe, just maybe, their good fortune in publishing was due, in part, to…good fortune, not mere talent.

"These are the same folks who railed against Borders," Kate had written to Marie to console her at one point.

"And then cried buckets when Borders closed," Marie had agreed.

"Oh, did you see that Melinda Milhouse has a blog post up about going the self-publishing route?" Kate wrote to Marie. Milhouse was a big paranormal author who'd been in the anti- self-publishing camp for a long time.

"Don't bother reading it. I did. Her 'tips' mostly consist of sneering at self-published authors having poorly written, poorly edited, poorly formatted products out there. And how she won't do that sort of thing with her effort."

"Uh…I've seen her blog. Does she still use reverse type – white on black?"

"Yeah, can hardly read it. And, yes, before you ask, there were a few grammatical errors—the old *it's* for *its* thing, mostly."

"Pot…"

"…meet kettle."

Kate found herself counting her blessings that she didn't need to face the mountain of work of self-publishing just yet, at least. She had an editor willing to get behind her once she finished this latest romance. And

Jim was okay. His leg was healing at a rapid rate, so much so that he was canceling the physical therapy after doing his follow-up checkup with the doc. He limped a bit, but with an elastic brace around his knee, he was able to function normally.

Part of his recovery might have been driven by his occupation. He seemed to be taking his "artistry" more seriously, retreating to the basement to paint every day—windows open regardless of the temperature—with a single-minded dedication that began to irk her again, now that she was sure he was healthy. It still felt as if he were poking fun at her, pretending to be as dedicated to his art as she was to hers. He talked about having a dream of images, black and white and yellow, with just a splash of red, and he was going to try to capture it. He went to Home Depot and bought cans of Canary Sun, Inkwell Ebony, Clothesline White, and Vintage Ruby, asking her to help him carry them to the basement. While he cranked up the music and began painting, she brooded.

Who was she trying to kid? She wasn't producing art. She was producing entertainment. She bent her nose to the grindstone and churned out more of *Wishful Thinking*, hoping to finish it soon so she could devote herself to *The March of Time*. It called out to her now, and she loved that feeling of yearning to create something. She spent all her writing time, even as she typed out Jake and Belinda's tale, thinking about Beatrice Rutherford and Zelda and Scott, particularly those horrible years when they were trapped...in Zelda's madness, Scott's seven-year struggle with *Tender Is the Night*, with the need to support his wife, with her desire to be sent to a state facility so he wouldn't have to work so hard to pay for her care. It was a real prison for them. The prison of requited love. Of idealized love.

CHAPTER NINETEEN

THE MARCH OF TIME by Beatrice Rutherford
My, but Baltimore was hot. Hotter than New York or Alabama, really. At least in New York there was the promise of ice-cooled drinks or cloyingly cool cinemas. And Alabama — why, being out in the country always seemed to bring the promise of rain-scented air somewhere. But Baltimore? Brick row houses trapping the heat. Concrete walkways reflecting it up at you. Dank odiferous hallways with electric fans throwing more hot air your way — it was enough to make one despair.

By this time in their lives, despair was a constant companion of the Fitzgeralds. Zelda at Phipps, Scott ensconced with Scotty at La Paix. That name just made a mockery of what their lives were really like. Anything but peaceful. The kind of dark turmoil that turns a soul away from God.

I think that started to bother me, too, their "Godlessness." I always knew they weren't church-going types. And truth to tell, my Baptist days seemed like a gauze-covered memory to me by then. I'd become too sophisticated for all that holy rolling. But I guess I did tend to think of them as still "spiritual" folks, like me, believing in...something. Now I have my doubts. And it worries me. You need to believe. It's what saves you. I know it saves me in the dark night when I lie there thinking of my Jeremy and what I lost. More and more I think of that and yearn so much for the sweet communion of later marriage, the tenderness I see in it, the gentle understanding, the sweet acceptance of flaws and overlooking of faults, the union that makes one of two.

I find myself talking to Jeremy more and more these days, sharing with him my thoughts on the poor Fitzgeralds, kind of smugly telling him how we never would have made those mistakes, him so sensible and me so responsible. No, sir, we wouldn't have squandered our money and youth on all the silly partying and traveling and such they engaged in. Oh, maybe a jaunt here or there, Jeremy. I know you would have liked to take me places with you, especially after getting to see France yourself. Why, now I did get to see it! And it was beautiful, too, probably a long sight better than what you saw. I was at the Mediterranean end, you see, with sunshine and glittering water just a diamond necklace glowing around you every single day. And warmth that felt like bath water, embracing you. Oh, Jeremy, you would have loved that, especially after the dreary parts you saw with the fighting.

And maybe you and me, we would have been the good ones, enjoying the freedom the time offered us but not turning our backs on the good old things, the truth and loyalty and wisdom. Maybe we'd have been those who'd held on, who'd been solid and sure to guide the world through the inferno to come. I came to realize I was a little red hen myself, and blush more and more thinking of the partying I joined in because it just felt so good to be part of something. Now I looked back on some of the movies that capture those times, not the talkies but the beautiful silent pictures, and I'm embarrassed for us, our whole generation. My, what will people think in days to come? They'll see through us for sure as children, silly children using the excuse of the War to do whatever thing we wanted to do at the moment we wanted it. Oh, Jeremy.

The poor Fitzgeralds only seemed to enjoy life in spurts now, like frames in a movie. There was an awful time, as I've said already, a time when she nearly threw it all away on that silly man, Jozan was his name. My God, but I had to control myself over that. I could barely look at her then. Here she had a handsome fellow, a man of great intellectual beauty, and someone others wrote about, talked about…and she fell for some aviator type like a cheap floozy from a dime novel. I know I've mentioned this already, but it was momentous, something hard to forget. What a betrayal! A betrayal of true love, most of all. I think that's what bothered me most, seeing how hard it was for these two to stay together, to stay faithful. If they couldn't do it…

I wouldn't think on it too much at the time except in a sort of judgmental scowling way, and, yes, I know it was hypocrisy given I'd nearly thrown myself into sin with R. But don't we all fall prey to that holier-than-thou disease from time to time? I was no saint. I was muddled, that was sure.

Thank the Lord, I was too busy during those days in France when he finally got down to real work to think about much except his stories. He had me typing and retyping to beat the band, until my fingertips felt raw from the work. But I didn't mind. I didn't mind at all when I saw what was coming from his mind and heart.

You see, he was brooding about that glorious Gatsby of his, that great American self-made man, while we were on Gaul's territory. It was, I believe, the best book he turned out, the best book I ever read, as I've already said. The feel of it...I don't think I could have captured in a million words what he put into that slim volume. It just said it all—laid bare the whole reckless devil-may-care life they'd led, but underneath it was this true love, this one true love story, Gatsby the knight, and his undeserving Lady, Daisy. Even that first version, the one his editor made him soften a bit, Gatsby was still a knight in my eyes, a big misunderstood galoot, a poor fellow so besotted he thought he could buy everything, even love.

But he did right by Daisy—Scott did, that is. He didn't make her into what I would have written, using Zelda as a guide. My, if I'd been the author, Daisy would have been exposed in all her wicked selfishness, with not a breath of sympathy blown her way by the reader.

Scott didn't do that, though. Daisy was pitiably sweet, and your heart ached for her knowing about her husband's infidelity, even if he was a cad and she could have chosen Jay. You just knew how those things went, making choices you think are wise, ruing them later. So you couldn't stop and be mad at her when you knew she hurt so bad she couldn't even see the joy in having a precious little baby girl.

So he wrote Zelda into Daisy in the best possible way, as a spoiled girl who couldn't be faulted for the spoiling done by others, and who couldn't be condemned for trying to make right the choices she'd made when she'd been too young to know better.

Did he feel that way about Zelda—that she shouldn't have chosen him? I think he was *both* Tom

Buchanan and Jay Gatsby in that tale, both the boorish husband and the romantic lover. And there was Zelda, always Zelda, and he was telling the world, see, she's a wonder, isn't she, you'd die for her if you could without a single regret, and you have to forgive her when she's naughty.

The real Zelda was trying this and that at the time, back there in France, frantic to chase madness away and trying to lock the door on it. At least in retrospect that's how it seems to me now. Unsuccessful, that was. Poor thing. I saw that in *Tender*, how he tried to show the world what a struggle it was for her, fighting those demons. Even then, even when he wrote about the worst in her, he presented her to the world as the creature to be pitied and cosseted and loved, and it was his character, Dick Diver, who ends up descending into decay. How he loved her!

Every book was a sacrifice on an altar to Zelda. Every story the same. Every permutation and characterization of Zelda was alluring, captivating, vulnerable even in her selfishness. Every portrait he wrote of her was a paean to his love. Don't forget that, world, I want to shout some times when I hear or read of this nasty bit of business concerning Scott's mistreatment of Zelda. Don't forget how he painted her, never with any of her flaws on display the way some authors treat their lovers, writing what amounts to a treatise of revenge, flinging the worst kind of mud at their wives, gussying it up as fiction when everyone knows full well who they're writing about, and the poor ladies have no recourse, no story they can tell that anyone wants to hear when the literary bully is hanging her dirty laundry — never his, mind you — out for all to see.

No, Scott wasn't like that. He always, always, always wrote about the best, most attractive parts of her, even when she was at her least attractive. He wasn't like that bear of a man, well, I won't mention his name, he with his hunting and bravado and getting in the way of those in the world who did the real fighting and the real winning.

And if Scott couldn't see to letting her have a life of her own — why, don't be thinking you can turn a man of one century into a man of another. It would be like trying to judge a medieval knight by today's standards — a fool's errand, and a cruel kind of foolishness at that. All men were like him at that time, thinking of themselves as the pillars of their personal fortresses, and their women as the maids they protected. Don't be thinking he should have done different by her. He did better than most! Much better than most.

I can't be too hard on Scott now, even though I did go through a spell when my inner pendulum had swung to being in her camp and her camp alone. But back then, back then when he was the sun around which we all orbited, why, you would look at her and couldn't help your lip from curling up and your Bible phrases about retribution and perdition coming to mind. When you saw her in her demented state, it was hard not to think, well, well, well, the chickens have come home to roost, have they not? It was mighty hard not to feel that way. Looking at her frazzled hair and oily skin, you thought, well, well, well, the mighty have fallen.

But those thoughts horrified me at night when talking to my Jeremy, and this is how my thinking really began to change about her. It was as if I could see him looking at me with those big sad eyes, disappointed in my pettiness. "Now, Bea, you know you shouldn't be judging her. You don't know what's in her soul. And haven't we all strayed?" He, the preacher's son, would be ready to forgive, eager to find a reason to do it. We all have strayed. My entire generation strayed, and I, like a sheep, went with them to the edge of the cliff, at least.

I tried thinking about what might be in her soul. I began to see it a little in those drawings she did. Pictures of herself that made you want to shake her and say, you're a pretty girl, Zelda, not this monster you've drawn. Maybe inside, though, she was a monster, and that was what ate her alive, that kind of thinking. She set about sobbing when Scott told her she couldn't dance that season the way she'd been pinning her hopes on. She looked at me and said, out of his earshot, "I wanted that one thing that wasn't his. I wanted something for me. Is that selfish, Bea?"

And bless her heart, I couldn't tell her it was selfish because it didn't seem so to me. Sure, I thought she should pay more attention to her wee one. But I'd seen how every part of their lives was scooped up by him, used by him, telegraphed to the world by him. And even if he did right by her in the telling of her tale, he still used it, used her to say his piece to the world. So I could see her wanting a small corner that was just hers to enjoy. I could see it and see his point, too, how he earned the money for them, how he provided, and he needed to keep that business of his safe from competitors, even if one was his wife. It was an awful dilemma for them both.

I think that's when my pendulum started swinging toward her, though. It's illness that brings out the best and worst of us, you see. And while he never wavered in his dedication to her care in the monetary sense — spending king's ransoms on her institutions when she kept begging him to put her in a public hospital where costs were lower—he could be cold in the individual sense, cruel at the personal level.

But I guess that, too, is a judgment when I know full well how sometimes it's a far sight easier to be dropping your dollar in the collection plate than to be helping that neighbor who annoys you so. We've all trod that path, an easier one than that which stretched before him.

It's the everyday that's hard, the noble quest hacked into a million steps, each one ordinary and without acclaim. I'd see Scott's face happy and determined when starting off to visit her, and then dark and angry after the visiting was done. The noble quest lifts you up, makes your heart soar. The everyday pulls you down.

So Scott's throwing money at the problem was probably a desperate way of expressing his love, and I bet that every time he got in the roadster to drive to the clinic in Europe and then in Baltimore, he was brimming with good thoughts on how he was going to show his affection to his afflicted wife. But then, face-to-face with her and her dementia, why, it did take some serious internal cheering and reflection to turn the Christian impulse toward charity into real action. It took practice.

I think Scott was feeling guilty, too, truth be told. He'd never held Zelda back from her wildness. He'd never tried hard to pull her back from the edge. He'd dived right in after her, literally in at least one case when she would swoop off a cliff into the sea below when we were all at Villa Marie, and he'd shiver and quake and then go after her. Part of him loved that about her. Part of him clung to it as a piece of their first excitement in love. So he must have felt like an accomplice in her downfall, and that's a mighty hard crime to face. Even I wondered if she could have been saved with a bit of discipline earlier on when the mind is softer and more malleable to learning right ways.

He couldn't face that, though. It was only natural to want to blame it all on her, even on her mother and father and their indulgent ways with their fair-haired child. My, he would bend my ear with those theories, all he'd read by the great Freud and Jung and how Zelda was just the archetype of the patients they'd treated. It put it all in a nice neat box for him

Of course, it was a box he was storing things in for the next big book, *Tender Is the Night,* that sad recitation of Zelda's madness and then Scott's own decline. That book troubles me no end. He took so long to write it – seven years at least by my recollection. And I never thought it was all that good in the writing. More in the storytelling.

See, here's the thing about *Gatsby*. I typed and retyped that for him and read it myself what must be dozens of times. And even I forget pieces of the plot, what really happened with Gatsby at the end and all that driving around and Daisy getting off free as a bird. It had some meandering to it, some feeling of scenes strung together to make a whole. But I remember the sense of it always, the beautiful, longing sense of it. The time, the songs, the way those characters felt about things. That's writing, not just storytelling.

But with *Tender,* I remember how Mrs. Diver goes mad and gets better and Dr. Diver falls for the young actress and there's sunshine and shadow and Dr. Diver ends up on the descent while his wife climbs out of her hole. So I remember the storytelling, not the writing really, except for some flashes here and there.

Maybe it was because he was so distracted. But the point is he took even this worst horrible time of Zelda's and he used that, too, like everything else that had been hers. And I guess if it had resulted in something like *Gatsby*.... But it resulted in a tale, a sad tale.

So it was hot in Baltimore when we were there, and he was in a mood fit to be tied, drinking to beat the band, trying so hard to get it all back — everything from Zelda and him to the writing. And poor little Scotty getting spoiled and raised in a capricious way. And me beginning my long reflection on what I'd been doing with my own life and whether Jeremy would approve.

And Zelda...well, she surprised even me. Zelda started to get better.

CHAPTER TWENTY

IT SNOWED AGAIN. Big, fat, wet flakes. When she saw them rushing from the sky, she took personal offense and growled at the heavens.

"I can't stand this anymore," she said to Jim over breakfast that morning. "I'm going crazy."

"It is a late snow," he said, as if apologizing for the weather.

"Let's go see Becky," she said, getting up to put her mug in the sink. "It's really spring down there. I want spring. Let's go away somewhere together — just you and me."

After a pause, he said, "Can't."

She knew why he couldn't before he even said it. "Can't or won't?"

"Have to finish this painting and ship it off. I promised."

Her hands fisted, her lips pursed. Painting. His painting. Hadn't his accident taught him anything? The universe was telling him to stop!

"Jim, if I don't get out of here —" she motioned to the window, gray panes overlooking a gray landscape as soft snow smothered them " —I will go freakin' crazy! I can't stand this anymore. I can't stand it!" She practically stomped her foot for emphasis. Didn't he see it really was driving her mad? Had that happened to Zelda? Had she felt imprisoned by Scott's expectations?

"I can't do this anymore," she whimpered, not even sure what the "it" was — writing romance to support them, staying here, staying Kate-and-Jim.

He stood and placed his mug in the sink, too, but with such a thunk she thought he'd broken it. He leaned on the sink, staring outside.

"You said the same thing before we moved here. You were going crazy in Maryland, remember?" His tone was low and angry.

"Thanks," she said, remembering. *Thanks for reminding me how weak I am.*

After they'd visited his grandfather that one summer, she'd actually been the one to broach the subject of moving. Vermont seemed so safe, so far from all the horrible worry of living. Jim had seen to everything with a zeal that had been lacking in his other endeavors. He'd found this house, he'd negotiated with the real estate agent, he'd gotten them settled. And those first years, she'd felt so safe and protected, so cared for.

She sucked in her lips, sucked up her hurt. She wouldn't cry. She'd be strong. "I am not happy here. I want to move." She crossed her arms and stared at his back, but he didn't turn around to face her.

After a long pause — Jim could be incredibly quiet, not responding for long minutes to an accusation or a compliment — he finally just repeated "not happy here," and she knew precisely its meaning. Not happy here...or anywhere?

It was something she'd thought herself. Was her urge to move merely a case of grass-is-greener yearning, the sense that a move, any move, would mean better pastures, brighter skies?

Well, yes, because brighter skies were guaranteed anywhere but here. Literally.

The rest, she couldn't ponder because it struck too close to the vulnerable part of her heart. Maybe she was unhappy because of other things? Because of Jim? Again, she wondered…what would her life be without him? She'd been devastated to think that when she'd found him on the basement floor, when she'd waited in the ER to find out he was all right. But now that he was here, safe, the same Jim, she was pondering the unponderable once more.

A pang of intense sadness hit her as she looked at him now, wishing he'd carry her back home, that he'd just pick her up and whisper in her ear that she was his first concern, that he'd protect her.

But from what?

She had to face that alone. She had to figure out who Kate was, alone. Not Kate-and-Jim. Just Kate.

So she went by herself. A long weekend, she said, when he dropped her at the station a day later. That's all she needed. Just a long weekend soaking up more spring.

But it was a different kind of getaway for her, and maybe it would be longer than a "long weekend." Jim didn't know it, but this trip was a test for her. On this trip, she would imagine there was no coming back. And maybe she wouldn't.

Jim didn't seem to pick up on any of this. He was on Cloud Nine with his "art" sale. And the paper had gotten hold of the story—had interviewed him. He'd even managed not to say anything dishonest or silly. He'd just talked about how much he enjoyed painting, what a great "liberating" experience it was, and how he was glad if his work gave someone pleasure.

He'd smiled and hugged her at the station, as if everything was all right between them and their previous argument had blown over.

It broke her heart.

❧

The next day, Kate was on a different planet. Or at least it felt that way to her. She'd left Vermont covered in damp, melting snow and arrived in a Baltimore bedazzled by greenery.

Becky, cutting roses in her garden, the very picture of a gardener with sunhat and gloves and pretty basket, turned up to her, squinting in the bright light of the day.

"We all create our own prisons, you know."

"What?" Kate had just shared her frustrations about Jim, her own writing, the Rutherford story, her agent. She'd not revealed how she thought of this visit as a test of her relationship.

Becky stood up, plopping her clippers into the basket with the vivid flowers, and sat on the garden bench next to her sister. Becky's garden was a wonder, a patch the size of a tennis court filled with flowers for every part of the blooming season, from early spring hyacinths to late blooming mums and sedum.

"Well, look at Bob and me. Sometimes we would like to take a vacation, get away, go to the beach. But money's tight." She spread her arms around. "Because of this. We love this place, but it can get pricey what with mortgage, taxes, college bills still being paid, upkeep. So it creates restraints on us. But we love it. Wouldn't give it up. We've talked about moving someplace cheaper, smaller. We don't want to. So, in a way, this is our prison. But it's one we've built and we've chosen."

"You think that's what I've done? Built a prison for myself?" Kate recoiled from the idea.

"You've made choices, haven't you?" Becky's tone turned brittle, as if she'd stored up these things to say. "You've decided to live full-time as a writer when plenty of folks do it on the side until they get a foothold."

"I have a foothold — my romance stuff!"

"You know what I mean — until they can essentially live the writer's life, not doing anything else."

"But if Jim worked —"

"You just told me about his art sale, honey. He's bringing in money."

"I mean steady work. He can do it, you know. He used to do it until I started making money with my romances."

"Why do you expect more of him than you do of yourself?" Becky leaned forward, not looking at her sister, her hands between her legs, the basket at her feet. "I think you're setting up this job thing as a test."

Kate warmed even more. If only Becky knew how right she was.

"Does he love you enough? All right, that's a legitimate question for a wife to have. Does he care as much as I care, what's the depth of his feeling, that sort of thing. Just don't make it a test."

Despite her sister's accuracy, Kate flushed with irritation at how petty Becky made it all sound, as if Kate were playing a game. "How else do you tell? I mean, anything you do to find out is a test of some kind."

"I don't know," Becky said after a long pause. "Maybe all of your time together is that test. The long march of years," she said with mock drama. "The crawl of time."

"Please."

"You're the writer, not me," Becky kidded.

"I just wish…" What did she wish for?

Becky looked up. "What?"

Kate shook her head. "I don't know. I guess I figure I could be a great writer if I didn't need to worry about the next check. I'd be free to write what I wanted to, and maybe I'd write something lasting, something worthwhile, something…sophisticated."

Becky snorted and stood, going over to a new patch that needed weeding. She set about the task.

"You are sophisticated already. And I think your writing is pretty damn great as it is."

"I appreciate that. But it's not, I'm not, you know, respected."

Becky stopped and looked at her, peering through steel-slit eyes. "Will you please stop this? You think you're not sophisticated, but what you really want is to be accepted by a bunch of folks like that Ranier person. And she's not sophisticated. She's a snob. There are probably dozens just like her. And you want their respect? Let me tell you something — there's a big difference between being sophisticated, having decent taste, and being a snob. A sophisticate can tell you why she likes Bach more than Handel. Someone with decent taste just happens to prefer Bach and Handel to some cheesy guitar strummer but can't really tell you why. And a snob is someone with decent taste who feels superior — either implicitly or explicitly — to those he perceives don't have it, even though he himself has nothing beyond the most shallow understanding of the things he holds dear, only knowing that they set him apart from the rabble. In fact, I'll go out on a limb here and say that most snobs probably reflexively dislike anything that's popular."

Kate couldn't help it—she burst out laughing. "Look at you, Ms. Font of Wisdom! Where did you come up with that?"

"Parenting. High school is the most caste-driven universe there is. And when your kids are dealing with snobs—except in their case it's the ones who swoon over Green Day and look down on Taylor Swift fans—you have to help them get through the weeds, so to speak."

"Ouch. So you're saying I'm acting childishly?"

"If the shoe fits...."

"You don't think the rabble can be snobs, too?"

Becky twisted her mouth to one side. "Good point. Yeah, they can. In that case, the reflexive dislike is for what high-art aficionados like, with no understanding of it or what they themselves like. It's a complicated topic."

"Maybe you should write a paper on it."

But Becky didn't respond to that, going back to her gardening, finally coming up for air to take another break in what seemed like decades—sun-dappled decades filled with time-stopping serenity—plopping herself next to Kate on the bench again, taking up where they'd left off.

"Look, I wish I could get it through that head of yours that you need to respect yourself, and to hell with the rest. It's a cliché, I know. But it's true. People with our backgrounds—working-class parents, first to go to college in the family—I think we always tend to think there are a whole bunch of folks more sophisticated than us. But I've come to the conclusion sophistication is really understanding. And if you have a deeper understanding of a topic—say, of the books you read and love, of classical music, country music or whatever—you qualify. I like sophisticated people. I loathe snobs."

They sat silently for a while, Kate mulling Becky's words, wishing she could internalize them, start living them, and wondering if they were really true at all. Then she changed the subject, commenting on a new housing development she'd gone by on her way to her sister's, a happy topic for both of them. They loved talking about interior design, even if neither could afford to buy new furniture, and they shared tidbits on crafty and inexpensive things to brighten a home.

"You know, every time I see neat little houses like that, all in a row, cars outside, a few kids playing, I think to myself how wonderful their lives must be, and I wish I could be them." Kate sighed.

"Maybe they think the same thing when they drive past your place!" Becky said, a smile in her voice.

"Well, certainly when they drive past yours," Kate added.

"And wouldn't they be surprised!" Becky stood, grabbing her basket of cut flowers. "C'mon. You can help me arrange these so they look delightful. We'll put them in the window. Folks who drive by will be dazzled. They will be sure to think the happiest and most sophisticated people in the world live here and be green as a frog with envy."

As they walked to the house, Kate finally told Becky that she did view this visit as a test—of herself.

"I can't stand Vermont. Not one more second. I want to live back here. And Jim, he just doesn't get it." To her surprise, she stopped and started crying.

Becky enveloped her in a big hug, letting the basket of flowers drop to the ground.

"Oh, honey," she said, comforting her sister. But as soon as Kate's tears had stopped, Becky tipped her face up, hand under her chin and said the same thing Jim had said to her earlier: "You'd wanted to move there, remember?" But her voice was quiet and nonjudgmental, just a reminder, not an accusation. So, as uncomfortable as it was to admit, Kate could nod yes.

"But it's over. I want to break up with Vermont." She managed a weepy smile.

Becky tilted her head and peered at her. "Fine," she said at long last. Don't confuse breaking up with the state with breaking up with your husband." She stepped away and picked up the flower basket. "Tell you what — let's go looking at houses tomorrow. There's a bunch of new developments around here with Open Houses on the weekends. It'll be fun."

ৡৢৡ

It was another week before Malcolm got back to her, and by that time, Kate was nearly ready to abandon him as an agent. She'd had enough of that sort of treatment — the glow of affection as the contract was being signed, followed by neglect and dismissal. She'd even written up the termination email, but when she'd told Jim about it after coming home, he'd tamped down her concern.

"You've had this fellow for how long — a few weeks?"

"A little longer."

"Not long enough to make that kind of decision."

She and Jim — they were coexisting in some sort of uneasy truce, not saying much to each other. She'd returned with nothing settled in her mind, nothing clear except, perhaps one thing: finding out who Kate was didn't necessarily mean moving beyond Kate-and-Jim. It meant standing up for what she wanted, even to herself.

And she was so busy meeting her editor's deadline that she had little time for existential crises. The urgency of their problems now seemed replaced with…what had Becky called it? The March of Time. No, that was Beatrice Rutherford's title for her memoir.

When Jim did speak, it was to tell her he'd paid a bill or taken care of a repair or some other household chore that had required a cash outlay. The implicit message: I'm providing for us with my "art" income.

Kate struggled with her feelings. She thought of her sister's advice. She kept lecturing herself on counting her blessings, thinking, as her sister had suggested, of the people who might drive by her house wishing they could live there.

Except she really couldn't imagine that. Their home was an extremely modest Cape Cod, the shingles a little dingy, the yard a bit worn, the driveway in need of repaving. Jim was good at fixing things and had done a lot to it. But there was more, always more on the list, often outstripping their finances more than his energy. Maybe she was too materialistic! Her home would be a castle to someone in real poverty!

It wasn't that she'd been raised in luxury. Her parents had been working class, her father working at the steel plant, her mother a housewife most of the time, until she started working part-time when Kate and her sister were in high school. That money had helped pay for both their community college degrees, and the work had come in handy when their father passed away suddenly of a heart attack during those years. Their mother had started working full-time after that until her death.

Maybe that was Kate's problem. Maybe she felt adrift because her parents were gone now, both leaving this earth suddenly—her father from a heart attack, her mother from cancer. She and Kate had both been shattered on each occasion, but they'd not really gotten into big soul-baring sessions over it. There'd been too much practical "stuff" to attend to—helping their mom pick up the pieces, then sorting out the financial picture after their mother's death, selling her modest split-level in a nearby suburb. Who had time to grieve? The business of life kept pushing in.

The business of publishing now pushed in. Malcolm's email was short and mysterious: *You available this afternoon for a call?*

Of course she was. She responded immediately and waited on pins and needles until the appointed hour, hands clammy as she wondered if he'd stand her up.

As it was, he was ten minutes late, and she was about to telephone him, when the phone rang, Caller ID showing his number.

"So, what's up?" she asked after a few quick pleasantries.

"I have something you need to think about. I spoke with Ranier today—"

Ranier? Why speak to her?

"—and told her we had a manuscript ready to roll using the Rutherford story as a skeleton. I told her she couldn't do a thing with the pages she had. She was not cooperative."

"Why'd you call her in the first place?" Kate asked, confused and angry. Was he selling her out, trying to appear "collegial" to fellow agents? Maybe he hoped to land on Ranier's firm.

"She'd not adequately responded to my email. I needed to make sure she knew she couldn't move forward with what she had." He paused, telling someone in his office he'd call someone else back, then continued: "She believes the Rutherford papers are authentic and in the public domain, and, as such, she can do whatever she likes with them. So I told her she might be in for the embarrassment of her life, that you had a fictional tale based on this story, and that she must have misunderstood you when you met originally. Beyond the embarrassment, however, would be the cost of litigation—if it came to that."

"What did she say?" Kate desperately tried to remember the details of her conversation with Ranier about the Rutherford papers.

"Not much. She tried to sound unconcerned, as if she didn't care that much. But I think she'll back off now. I don't think she wants to be the butt of a literary joke, which is what I tried to make her see. I think that would worry her more than a lawsuit, actually. I told her I already had interest from a few editors eager to read it, and it was in their hands."

"Is that true?" Kate sat back, breathless with hope.

"Yes." He mentioned two names she'd heard of— editors at Doubleday and Simon & Schuster, people who'd handled serious fiction.

She didn't know how to feel. Part of her was ecstatic, over the moon, beyond happy. All this time, all these agents, she'd waited for this—serious attention from serious editors. But it was with a story based on Beatrice Rutherford's tale, not her own.

"Kate, I really wouldn't be surprised if we got an offer—maybe even a pre-empt—before the week is out."

She sat back in her chair. Was this her work—or Beatrice Rutherford's?

"Kate?"

"Yes. I'm here. I'm…flabbergasted, I guess."

"When an offer comes in, there might be some, oh, fuss when the deal is announced. After all, Ranier announced hers already. We'd need to get our ducks in a row...."

He went on to suggest a public relations strategy, a statement from her attesting to the fictional nature of the story, even though it was based on some "notes" she'd found, the origins of which were murky. And that Ranier must have misunderstood her when she first presented the papers to her. True enough...to a degree.

"You said Ranier was confused about *Wuthering Heights,* too, right?" he prodded.

"*Jane Eyre,*" she said, remembering how she'd confided the story of her meeting with Ranier to Malcolm when they'd had their first conversation. And then she remembered Becky's words about a sophisticate — someone who understood beyond a shallow level.

"Well, we won't embarrass her with that story — she'd deny it anyway — but we can certainly say that she seemed very busy and was possibly distracted when you talked. I can remind her privately of the Bronte mix-up. She wouldn't want that kind of thing floating around." Kate had also told him of the other client coming in to sign papers while she was there, and he brought that up, too, suggesting he could use it to hint that Ranier' attention had been divided during the meeting, understandable in this frenetic business.

"My guess is Ranier will back down. She'll put her tail between her legs and skulk away, withdrawing the papers from the publisher. I'll say something magnanimous about her, about how all agents are busy, it was only a natural mistake that she thought you were talking about something other than your own story."

"I—I feel like a fraud," Kate whispered. Her goal was within reach—a good contract for a literary book from a decent publisher, but she felt suddenly like Jim, with his wall paint and canvases. She felt bourgeois, clumsy, awkward.

She heard Malcolm sigh. "Look, Kate, who's to say who's real and who's a fraud? Don't get me wrong—I'm not saying you are. I'm just saying that you're as real as you think you are. You came up with the story of how things end for Zelda and Scott. That's your story. That's the important part. Your story. Tell your story."

"Okay," she said, her hand clenched tight around the receiver.

A few minutes later she was off the phone, staring at the backyard, listening to the sounds of the neighborhood. Jim was painting. She could hear his music selections wafting up to her—Marc Cohn's "Walking in Memphis" was on now.

"Tell me are you a Christian child?"
And I said "Ma'am I am tonight"

She could hear children screaming with delight as they bounced on a trampoline nearby, the springs a rhythmic squeak behind their chatter; they were grabbing moments from Vermont's miserly spring. She could hear a TV faintly in the distance tuned to news.

She wanted to go and talk to Jim, but she knew where any conversation would lead. She wanted to confess her fears—that *Wishful Thinking would* be successful, forcing her to write more of the same, that the Rutherford project would sell, but would make her feel like Jim and his art—a phony. That she'd never get home.

She could hear what he'd say, how he'd reassure her, tell her once again she was a good writer, and it would mean...nothing. Nothing if she didn't herself believe it. Why couldn't she believe it?

Tears welled in her eyes. She ran her fingers through her hair, shook her head. She stood and stretched, refused to cry. She walked swiftly to the dining room and grabbed her purse, then opened the basement door.

"Running to the store!" she shouted down, listened for Jim's answering "Okay," and left.

∾౿౿∾

She didn't drive to the store. She just drove. She found herself heading south of town. Driving south always calmed her, as if she were going to keep on driving until she reached home, imagining a seamless, winding highway — straight from her heart to her heart's desire.

The southern road led to the mall, a small group of shops with anchor stores a mere fraction of the size they'd be in real cities. She drove into the lot, parked, and got out, rushing into a Penney's. The place was virtually empty. She smelled new clothes, remembering how much she'd loved shopping with her mom, how bonding over a rack of new clothes soothed hurt, put disagreements to rest.

She walked the length of the mall, staring in shop windows, feeling lonely in the empty space. Where was everyone? It was if a natural disaster had occurred, and they were the sole survivors.

She was about to get what she felt she deserved. Only she felt she didn't deserve it. Not this. But Malcolm had said it was her story, really. All that mattered was her story. Tell that story.

She walked around and around and out again, to the car. Then she drove home a long way, back and forth and over and around the streets of their little town, the run-down sections, the more expensive blocks, the houses, like theirs, built more than fifty years ago and being kept up by new tenants.

Were people in these houses happy? Or were they in prisons, too? Did their inhabitants look out from their cells wishing they could be somewhere else, in some other house?

She'd thought of moving farther out into real countryside but had always nixed it because...because she was afraid if they were too far from any town, Jim would never look for work, using the commute as an excuse.

Just past the edge of town, her gaze landed on an old white house, back from the road. She pulled over and stared. A white house with a porch, no porch railing, just posts. She liked that, she'd always found that open look appealing, open to the outside with the embrace of shelter.... Nearby a clothesline was hung with laundry, triggering the smell of clean, wet cloth she'd not sensed in a long, long time. Her mother used to hang out clothes occasionally. Who did that anymore? Even she stuffed things in the dryer on warm, sunny days, too lazy to lug them outside. But maybe this house had a mud room where the laundry was located, making it easier...maybe this house made you into a better person, sure of yourself, with enough time to do things slowly, carefully, thoughtfully.

When she saw a woman stepping onto the porch, Kate quickly turned the key and drove off, feeling a bit guilty. Poor woman probably wondered who was sizing up her house—a burglar, perhaps, casing the joint?

By the time she got home, she'd not sorted out her feelings about *The Last Romantics* or her writing career, but she had decided on one thing:

"I want to put the house up for sale," she told a shocked Jim over a dinner of carryout pizza. "Now."

He was silent for a moment, then nodded. "And buy another one—where?"

"Home."

He nodded again, this time almost imperceptibly. He knew what home meant to her.

"You can look for a job there, okay? Like we talked about."

"Okay."

"And...and...maybe I will, too."

"Give up writing?" he asked, stunned. "Kate, that's kind of—"

"No. Don't say it. I know you think I'm a good writer. I appreciate that. But maybe I need to just stop relying on it for income." Maybe that was her prison. "Maybe I'll just work part-time. But then I can write what I want instead of..." Instead of writing what she thought the Raniers of the world expected her to write. Time wasn't her problem. Income wasn't her problem. She had to respect the Kate who wanted to write other things. Kate. Not Kate-and Jim. Not Kate-and-romance. Kate.

"...instead of what Alice wants you to write."

"Yes." *Yes.*

He hugged her and kissed her forehead. He held her hands and looked into her eyes, and she liked to think he was saying he understood, and that she wouldn't have to face that prospect because he would provide.

Later, she told him about the white house, the one she dreamed about, about hanging clothes on a line, and he smiled, nodding at each point. Then she surprised herself with quiet frankness: "I know you like it here. But you can look for work elsewhere. Just look in Maryland or somewhere near there—Pennsylvania, Virginia. Someplace warm," she said into the dark as they lay in bed together. "But we can come visit here. Do a ski vacation."

"You don't like to ski."

"I like hot chocolate."

She could feel his smile as his body relaxed next to hers.

"Talk to a real estate agent down there," he said after a few minutes.

"And Becky. I'll tell Becky to keep her eye out for us."

"We can rent at first."

"Sure. We could do that." And, after a pause, "I guess that's one advantage of not having steady work up here. No need to worry about losing a job."

She fell asleep dreaming of the white house.

CHAPTER TWENTY-ONE

KATE WAS LATE with finishing her manuscript. She'd already told Alice she'd have it in after deadline, and her editor seemed appeased if a little scolding: "I went out on a limb to give you this earlier slot, Kate." Kate reassured her she'd have no trouble making the new deadline—she was on fire to get this story finished, and its last details were finally falling in place in her mind. The problem with adding bears to a boat, she realized, is you had to deal with each one by the end of the ride. It took some thought.

Oddly enough, once Malcolm had shared the possibility of selling *The Last Romantics*, Kate found she no longer resented the time she spent on *Wishful Thinking*. It called to her. She genuinely liked Jake and Belinda and wanted to live in their world as she finished their tale. Suddenly, they felt real to her, not cutout characters from a formula romance. She lived and breathed with them, longed and loved. She wished she could be them, both of them—strong, mature Jake, and impulsive, confident Belinda. She wanted to live in their house.

She knew the difference between poorly done romance, where characters sounded as if they had thought balloons over their heads, and well-written stories where hero and heroine would be recognizable in real life. She stopped thinking of the implications of selling steamy romance, how it might lock her in to that genre for a while. She just enjoyed her craft as she wrote.

She thought she was going crazy.

As for Malcolm, well, a week in Publishing Universe equaled a month or longer anywhere else. She wasn't surprised when he didn't call with extravagant offers from the two editors he'd sounded so sure about. If anything, she now expected an email every day from him beginning "Sorry to report..." or the more succinct observation of a rejecting editor's note: "She's an idiot." Did editors know how agents talked about them to clients?

She did get an email from Malcolm, but it was just a report from his agency's legal department—they'd found not a single living relative of Beatrice Rutherford, no claim to her work. It was as if she didn't exist at all. Some of her guilt evaporated.

But on a Friday evening, two weeks after Malcolm had told her about the possible deals and one week before her new *Wishful Thinking* deadline, he called. Six-thirty. Unheard of. An agent working late on a Friday?

"Great news, Kate," he began, and her world changed.

Great news translated into one offer. No, there had been no pre-empt, no auction. One editor had passed, reluctantly, just not sure how to "market such a unique project." Kate and Malcolm both giggled over that—like her, Malcolm found it astonishing when editors admitted they didn't know how to actually sell books.

But the other editor—he was willing to pay an advance well beyond what she'd ever received for romance, well beyond what Jim had just received for his "fake" art.

"I think I can ratchet it up a bit," Malcolm told her. "After all, he knows I've not submitted it widely, so he's risking losing it if he doesn't pony up. Are you with me on that?"

"Absolutely!" she said with a confidence that seemed attached to someone else. What did she have to lose? It was a fake manuscript anyway. No, a fake real manuscript. Or maybe a real fake one. Who knew?

"He knows about the Ranier deal, by the way, and doesn't care. Might even add some publicity value—he knows controversy can help sell things, and he thinks this one would be a plus for the book."

Sort of like a book burning, Kate thought, remembering poor Jenny Deerborn's desire for attention for a good book stranded in the desert of spine-out general fiction.

Malcolm then went through the points he would try to win for her—retaining digital rights, but if that wouldn't fly, an extremely generous royalty rate with fixed termination terms so she could regain her rights if the publisher did little to keep the book in front of readers; a larger-than-usual split on subsidiary rights, especially dramatic rights; and cover veto power.

"You think you can get those?" she asked, breathless. She'd never had an agent give her so much information about negotiations. In the past, if she'd asked questions, they'd treated her with condescension.

"Hell if I know. But I'm certainly going to try. Hang tight. I'll let you know as soon as I know something."

And he did. The weekend passed, and late morning on Monday, she received an email with the subject heading: *deal terms attached.* He'd not gotten everything, but he'd snagged a few, and he'd upped the advance by a few percentage points. Her hand shook as she printed it out and went searching for Jim, finding him in the garage.

"I can't believe it," she said, as she explained what had happened. "My first big contract."

"Believe it, honey! You deserve it. You deserve all of it and more," Jim said with conviction. He hugged and kissed her, and for those long moments, she felt young again, as if they'd just fallen in love, and she was wondering if he cared as much for her as she did for him.

When they pulled apart, she noticed what he'd been doing when she'd come looking for him. His painting supplies, the paint cans, brushes, stirring sticks, rags — he was loading them up in the car, carefully placing them on an old tarp.

"What—" She pointed to his labor.

He shrugged, a little sheepishly, as if he were conceding a point and hadn't wanted her to notice. "If the house is going on the market, we've gotta clean it up."

Something tender and heartbreaking coursed through her. Tears came to her eyes, and she blinked them away. "Jim," she said on a whisper, reaching out to stroke his arm.

He smiled. "Gotta run before the dump closes for the day." Then, over his shoulder as he walked to the driver's side door, "Get some champagne!"

For the first time in a long time — maybe since the whirlwind days of high school and college when social life competed with studying — Kate felt things speed up. The contract was finalized, the deal announced, publicity began. Ranier did slink away, as Malcolm had predicted, but not before giving some quote to *Publishers Weekly* about Kate's misrepresentation of the manuscript to her, "perhaps understandable – she's a genre writer and doesn't know, obviously, how this part of publishing works, but lamentable since I'd spent precious time" on the project.

It dripped with condescension, so much so that Kate could actually laugh at it, along with Malcolm.

Becky and Bob promised a celebratory dinner for her, the next time she visited, which would be soon because Becky was intent on helping her find a house to move into "ASAP, before I get gray hair." Alice offered sincere, if slightly fearful, congrats—"*you won't abandon your romance fans, will you?*"—and the local public radio station interviewed her about the book when they'd never given her a nanosecond of attention for her dozen romance novels. Maybe because of the new deal, Alice all of a sudden found more time to give her to finish *Wishful Thinking*.

It now flowed easily from her fingers, Jake and Belinda like old friends, the danged sex scenes out of the way, only the final perils-of-Pauline rescue to be penned.

She flung bears out of the boat one after another....

Threatening note-writer to Belinda? Caught! Splash!

Belinda's disillusionment with her boss, the mayor? Looks for new job! Splash!

Jake afraid to ask Belinda about commitment? He mans up. Splash!

And finally...old life insurance policy on Belinda taken out by evil stepdad years ago.....

CHAPTER TWENTY-TWO

WISHFUL THINKING – CHAPTER THIRTY

The hopefulness of love. It made Jake feel as if anything were possible, as if he were really young again where life itself was new. It was a drug. Here he was, a man addicted to knowing, not guessing, opinions, and he was betting on Belinda's answer without knowing the full extent of her opinion.

Just this morning he'd given a client bad news, a successful businessman who hoped to throw his hat in the political arena. But survey results painted a bleak picture. The public wasn't on the man's side on the issues, and they didn't know much about him. That had been the only ray of light—if people had no opinion of the exec, he could try to shape it and possibly persuade folks to his point of view. A steep hill, but the fellow was ready to climb it.

As Jake had made the presentation, the man had grilled him relentlessly, trying to poke holes in the way Jake had framed the survey questions. But Jake had told him what he told them all: your best predictor of the future is the past. The more you can construct questions that ask people what they have done in the past, the more you'll be able to see what they will do in the future.

Everyone likes to think well of themselves, you see, he'd explained. And so they'll answer a question such as "Do you think schools need more funding?" with a resounding yes. But if you ask them if they've voted to increase education funding in the past election, you might get a different, more honest answer.

During that explanation, Jake had thought of Belinda and what her behavior predicted. She was young but loved being with him, even doing the quiet things he enjoyed. They'd gone to concerts, had dinner with his brother and his fiancée, watched football on Saturday afternoons, attended an art exhibit at a museum and made wild, crazy love whenever they had the chance. Step by step, moment by moment, they'd built something. She said with her actions she wanted to be with him. Now he had to take the leap and act on his "poll" results, throw his own hat in the arena.

From his last conversation with her, as they'd started planning another weekend away, he knew she was very clearly telling him she'd consider a marriage proposal. The doubts and fears were over. Her anger with him for hiring Sean was over. If anything, that might have led to a breakthrough in their relationship. No longer enamored with her boss, she was considering other work. Maybe even joining a polling firm about to open a communications division.

He strode into the outer office and briskly informed Barb to clear his schedule for the rest of the week. Before she could ask too many questions, he walked down to Brian's office where he found the fellow poring through financial spreadsheets. Without knocking, Jake entered and stood before Brian's desk.

"Something unexpected's come up. I'll be leaving town for a few days. I want you to keep pursuing these other ventures and provide me with a risk/benefit analysis by late next week if that's feasible. I'm especially interested in the communications division – what it would look like, how much it would cost, potential staffing," he said to Brian.

Brian brightened. "Sure. That's great. It sounds like you've really bought into this."

"And, let me know, honestly, whether Belinda Remington would fit into the mix."

If that surprised Brian, he didn't show it. "No problem. I enjoyed working with her on her mayor's project. Smart cookie."

What he didn't tell Brian, Jake thought as he walked back to his office, was the rest of his plan. Sell out his portion of Pandora to Brian. Get Belinda positioned so she had a fair shot at heading its new communications division. Then, pick up his youth where he'd left it before raising Chris – go sailing, get his Ph.D…start a family. His step lightened as he entered his office. Before completely crossing the threshold, he turned to his administrative assistant.

"Barbara, can you recommend a good jeweler in town?" he asked.

As inscrutable as ever, she didn't blink an eye at the request. "Freeman's, near the harbor," she said. "Been there forever."

"Thanks."

Before he headed out, Barbara handed him a thick manila envelope. "Oh, this came for you today," she said. Unopened, it was marked "Personal," and it was from Sean Castleton. His bill and his report. Jake quickly stuffed it into his briefcase and left, frowning. No need to look at that now. It brought back bad memories of his tiff with Belinda. Besides, he knew an electronic version was waiting in his email box, as well.

In a buzz of happiness, he picked out a ring, went home, threw clothes in a sports bag, and was on his way.

Several times on the road out of Baltimore, he thought of how he'd ask her. When he'd ask her. Keeping himself from blurting out the question when he first saw her would be a real challenge in self-control.

His drive went smoothly for an hour and a quarter. About forty-five minutes from his destination, the traffic gods scowled. A rolling backup on the turnpike turned into a dead stop. He flipped on a local traffic station to get the scoop. A trailer had overturned and spilled rice on the freeway. Expect half hour delays. Damn. He was stuck between exits with nowhere to go. The GPS gave no alternate routes he could reach easily. He punched in Belinda's number. It was after four. She was probably home packing.

"Hello?" she answered breathlessly, as if she were hurrying.

"Hi. It's me. I'm stuck in traffic. Rice on the freeway if you can believe it," he said, drumming his fingers on the wheel. Maybe it was a good sign—they threw rice at weddings, right?

"Don't worry about it," she said. "I'm in a mad rush. This will give me a little more time. "

"Did you get the reservations?" he asked. She'd volunteered to do that planning.

"You bet. Beachfront property. Hot tub. Stereo, full menu of cable TV options, modern kitchen," she said.

"Maybe we should just stay there permanently," he said. His car was completely stopped amidst a sea of vehicles. Some drivers had actually turned off their engines.

"We certainly can make some fond memories there," she purred. "I hope you brought that box you keep in your bedside table. And I hope it was full."

He smiled. "Oh, darn. I knew there was something I forgot," he teased.

"We can always stop and pick up more," she said without missing a beat. Then she proceeded to tell him in a sexy, flirtatious voice what she hoped to do with him that weekend. His excitement grew with each word.

"Stop," he said at last. "Unfair."

"Okay," she laughed. "But right now, I better get back to packing. I want to take a quick shower. Call me again when you get near the city," she said, "so I know when to expect you."

"You got it," he said and signed off. He turned on the radio again. Still calling for a fifteen minute delay. No progress there. He looked over to the passenger side and saw the manila envelope from Castleton poking from his briefcase. Keeping his peripheral vision on the movement of the cars around him, he grabbed the packet and thought of cramming it under the seat, out of Belinda's sight. Castleton was a sore subject.

What the hell...he opened it, started scanning.

Jake had to acknowledge that, whatever Sean Castleton's faults, he put together a neat report. Nearly ten pages of notes, organized into sections detailing each part of his investigation, were placed on top of the invoice, which itself wasn't unreasonable.

The car up ahead moved a little. Putting down the papers, Jake pulled up as well, only to be disappointed by another full-fledged stop. He grabbed the notes again.

It summarized the information Jake had given to Castleton at the outset, what the detective had gleaned from police and other sources, and his investigative technique.

Then, he listed the possible motivations for killing Payton and arranged under each one possible suspects. Most were easily eliminated. Castleton had rated each one from strong potential to moderate to neutral. The only one that rated even a moderately strong was "unknown political terrorist" which was a fancy way of saying "nutcase." Castleton had done a thorough job of summarizing other similar terrorist actions, but he noted at the end of that section that "most, if not all, of these activities were centered on issues of national, even global, significance, and a small-town New Jersey mayor with a low profile doesn't attract enough attention."

Out of the corner of his eye, Jake saw brake lights begin to flash way up ahead as cars turned their engines back on. He flipped on the traffic radio station. The blockage had been cleared. Traffic would be slow but moving in about five minutes.

He quickly turned to the few pages on Belinda. There wasn't much there. Sean had not been exaggerating when he'd said that she had no visible enemies. After listing possible motivations, Sean went through the handful of former colleagues and friends and rated them all with "weak" in the potential suspect area.

In the "conclusions" and "recommendations" section, Castleton noted that no suspects were obvious and that the shootings could be the result of "random violence" or some unknown motivation he had yet to identify.

"Prior to the client's desire to cease the investigation, Castleton Associates also found one person associated with Ms. Remington in the past whose whereabouts and motivations should perhaps be more thoroughly researched. Just before being told to shut down the case, we discovered that Ms. Remington's stepfather was living in New Jersey where he moved several years ago after being paroled from a California prison. He has a criminal record that includes some violence. However, due to the fact that we were told to stop the investigation, we never adequately pursued this lead."

An icy finger traced up Jake's spine. But the cars were moving, and he had to throw the papers on the passenger seat and concentrate on driving. Like the cars breaking free of the jam, his mind started to clear as he thought through the last bit in Castleton's report. And, the more he thought, the more uneasy he felt.

The abusive stepfather. Belinda and Rosemary both had barely known him. Their mother had divorced him. Perhaps a subsequent wife had filed charges, and that's how he'd landed in jail. But what could be the motivation? Revenge? Had Belinda ever reported him to the police when her mother had been married? Did he see Belinda as the reason the marriage broke apart?

Jake's throat went dry, his palms sweaty. As he picked up speed, his ideas picked up confidence.

He needed more information on the stepfather. Worrying Belinda, however, wasn't the way to do it. He retrieved Rosemary's number, then let it dial through on his Bluetooth. Be there, he silently prayed. Her voice came on the phone, and he went right to the point.

"Rosemary, I need you to do me a favor," he explained. "I'd like you to tell me everything you can about your stepfather. Everything."

"Jake? Where are you?" Rosemary asked. He could hear the kids. They were probably eating dinner. He'd interrupted them. But he couldn't worry about that now.

"I'm on my way to see Belinda," he said, turning his tone from urgent to friendly. Rosemary would be more helpful that way. "We're going away for the weekend." He peered ahead at the heavy traffic and hoped no more jams awaited him. "But back to your stepfather..."

"Oh. Yeah. Why do you want to know?" she asked. "Afraid crazy relatives will come back to haunt you guys?"

"Did you know your stepfather is in Jersey? Is there any reason – any reason in the world, no matter how far-fetched – that he would want to harm Belinda?"

As he said the words, the reality of them sank in. Of course it had to be him. How perfect. Belinda was in a public position. Focus on trying to kill her in public and everyone assumes you're going after the public official – the mayor. Very shrewd. Very clever. Except he'd tried to kill her when she was alone, too. The train station. Why? What was driving him?

"He was an abuser, like we told you, going after our mom," Rosemary said sadly and lowly, probably so the kids wouldn't hear. "We didn't really know him that much. We stayed out of his way. Belinda probably even knew less about him than I did. He's in Jersey now?" Her voice shook, telling him how awful the man was.

"Did Belinda ever get him into trouble – even inadvertently – with your mother, the police?"

"No, no," Rosemary said. "I swear there were days when we just stayed in our rooms to avoid running into him. I probably wouldn't even recognize him if I saw him today."

If Rosemary wouldn't, Jake was sure Belinda couldn't either.

"Think, Rosemary. Anything. Did he remarry? Did Belinda get some money that should have gone to him?"

"I don't know, Jake. I really tried to shut out that part of my life after he was gone. It was a brief marriage, thank God. It was like a blank spot on the tape, if you know what I mean," she said. "Wait a minute. I can look through some stuff. I'm a pack rat. And after our mother died, I kept everything. I was always afraid we'd need some official papers, so I saved it all. I could look through that, and some scrapbooks. Maybe something will come to me."

"Can you do it now?" Jake asked, insistently.

"All right. I'll call you back in about ten minutes," she said. "I'll just find the stuff and go through it with you on the phone."

"Okay. Thanks."

◈◈◈

After Jake had hung up with Rosemary, he glanced over at the cover sheet on Castleton's report and phoned the first number on the letterhead. Voice mail. He left an urgent message. He called information and retrieved Castleton's home number, feeling helpless stuck in bumper-to-bumper traffic. Voice mail again. Damn! He left another urgent message. As soon as he hung up the phone, however, it rang. Jake answered while maneuvering into the fast lane. He had to get to Belinda as soon as possible.

"Castleton here," the detective's voice said a little coldly. "I was on another call when you phoned. Anything wrong?"

"I read your report. Very thorough. I want you back on the case," Jake said through gritted teeth. "I need your help right away."

"Doing what? They caught the guy," Castleton said, referring to the Avenging Gunman.

"I think you and I know that's not the guy," Jake said over the noise of the traffic. "Do you have any contacts at motor vehicles?"

"A few."

"Get hold of one. Right now. Find out if Buck Gilmore owns a dark SUV. And anything else you can get on him in fifteen minutes."

"I've got other clients," Castleton argued.

"I'll pay you double for the time. I need the info right away." Jake was practically shouting at the man.

"All right."

Jake cut the phone's connection and drove, zooming over the limit without caring. He had an intense, gut-wrenching fear growing in his stomach. They'd all been so blind. He thought of calling Belinda, but he didn't want to worry her until he knew more.

Oh, what the hell, he thought, he had to try. He spoke her name, and the phone dialed.

Jake felt the blood drain from his face as he listened to Belinda's phone ring and ring and ring before clicking over to voice mail. He left a brief message. "It's Jake. Call me as soon as possible. It's urgent. And don't let anyone in your apartment. No one. I'll call you before I come in."

As soon as he hung up, Rosemary called him back, her voice shaky and frantic. She sounded as if she was crying.

"What is it?" he asked when she identified herself, almost afraid to hear.

"One million dollars," Rosemary said. "Why didn't I see it before? Why didn't I check? I just wanted to forget. I...I..." She broke off, too overcome. Rick came on the phone after first telling his wife that it wasn't her fault.

"It's an old insurance policy," Rick explained. "One of those low-payment deals for a high payoff on kids. Really kind of a scam if you think of it. It's highly unlikely a kid would go before their parents. Anyway, Rosemary's mother apparently bought into it and bought two policies when she was married to Buck – one for Rosemary and one for Belinda. It has a double indemnity clause, too."

Jake could have groaned. The train. If Belinda died in an accident, Buck would collect double.

"Rosemary has a copy of the policies?"

"No. Only the one on her. Which makes her think the other one is still active. Rosemary said she remembers receiving a letter from Buck's second wife, who had been making the premium payments like a good little woman, asking her if she wanted to continue the policy. She got the letter when she turned eighteen. She wrote back and said, no, she didn't want it. Cancel it."

"But what about Belinda's?" Jake's knuckles were white on the steering wheel as he took in the information. Belinda had been walking around with a two million dollar price tag on her head.

"Rosemary doesn't know. She assumed the woman wrote to Belinda, too. But there's the possibility that she didn't. By the time Belinda turned eighteen, he might not have even had the same wife."

"Thanks," Jake said, not knowing what else to say.

"Do you want me to make some calls? Do you think Belinda's in danger?"

"I don't know."

"Rosemary just tried to call her," Rick said ominously. "She didn't answer. Aren't you two going away?"

Jake inhaled sharply. She'd said she wanted to take a shower. Maybe that's where she was when he called. Please, God, let her be in the shower, let her be all right.

"I'm only about twenty minutes away now," Jake reported. "I'll call you back if I need you."

He was about to hit the speed dial number for Belinda when the phone rang again. It was Castleton getting back to him.

"Bingo," the detective said with a tone of self-satisfaction. "He leases a Jeep Cherokee. Navy blue. And I got more, too."

"Tell me," Jake said, while fear gripped him.

"He's been married for the past five years to a Sally Matuchi from Jersey City. But Ms. Matuchi filed charges against him a month ago and served divorce papers on him about the same time."

"Do you know why he was in prison?" Jake asked, softly. His voice could barely speak the words.

"Assault with a deadly."

"And he got out?"

"I know. Go figure."

"What are you doing now?" Jake asked. "Listen, you've got to head to Belinda's apartment. Call me when you get there. I'll let her know you're coming. Just stay with her until I get there," he said. By his reckoning, it was a toss-up which of them would arrive first. Castleton was cross town from Belinda's apartment.

"Okay. No sweat."

Jake tried Belinda again. The phone rang and rang, then the voice mail kicked in again. No answer. He looked at the clock. Six-fifteen. He would be there by six-thirty if he hurried. He left a message saying Sean Castelton was on his way over, and he'd explain why when he got there. He called Rick back and told him what was up, urging him not to alarm Rosemary, but asking him to notify the New Jersey police.

He tried her exactly every three minutes as he made his way through crowded city streets, cursing other drivers and himself. No answer. Each time. No answer. His heart was in his stomach.

Jake died a half dozen times before he reached Belinda's apartment. She hadn't answered the phone at all when he'd called, and it was way past the time she'd be out of the shower. He left his car double-parked out front, scanning the other automobiles to see if he recognized Castleton's. Not seeing it, he made his way into the building. With dismay, he realized the doorman was not on duty.

He also realized that the building was dark. The electricity was out. Another bolt of fear shot through him. His hands were sweaty and his head throbbed as he considered the possibilities. Buck could have cut the lines, pulled a fuse.

Bypassing the dead elevator, Jake started running up the stairs two at a time. When he reached the second floor, he heard a door open above him. Holding his breath, he listened.

To Jake's horror, he heard Belinda's voice, strained, nervous and afraid, on a floor above him.

"Let me help you, Buck. I can give you that money. This is too risky. Much better for me to help..."

"Shut up and keep walking," a man's voice growled. Jake's hands automatically clenched into hard fists. He let his breath out slowly, trying to keep his presence hidden as he decided what to do. When he heard them moving up the stairs, he started following, quietly, walking on the edges of the steps. He heard Belinda stumble, then cry out.

"Ow!" she said. "You don't need to be so rough." She sounded on the verge of tears, and Jake's stomach twisted.

The door opened below. Castleton, thought Jake. He was catching up. Quickly, Jake flew down the steps to intercept the detective. He could hear Buck and Belinda stopping, a muffled cry coming from her mouth.

"Did you check the fuse box?" Jake said loudly as he looked at Castleton and gestured up above. "I already looked at the wiring on the first floor."

Castleton caught on to the charade quickly. He nodded his head. "Yeah," he said in an equally booming voice. "No dice. Guess we better look at that mainframe box upstairs."

Jake watched as Castleton pulled a gun from his jacket pocket and held it with both hands. He nodded at Jake to move on up, along the wall behind him, while looking up to see if Buck was peering down at them. "Fifth floor, right?" Castleton asked.

"Uh-huh," Jake agreed, following the detective's lead. He heard Buck mutter a soft curse above.

As the two men trudged upstairs, Jake picked up the small sounds that indicated Belinda and Buck were on the move, as well. When they reached the fifth floor, Castleton opened the door wide as if they were leaving.

"Got the flashlight?" Castleton asked. "It's getting kind of dark."

"Yeah," Jake answered, only able to croak out monosyllables, his throat choked with worry.

Castleton let the door whoosh shut while they waited on the landing. In a few seconds, they both heard Buck.

"Come on, get going. Hop to," the man said with fierce anger in his voice. "Not much time. Those jokesters'll probably have the juice running soon."

Jake and Castleton crept up along the wall, keeping their presence hidden. They were probably two floors below Belinda and Buck, Jake guessed by the sound of the footsteps echoing in the stairwell.

Just as Buck and Belinda reached the top floor...Jake's cell phone chirped.

The mood in the stairwell electrified. It was as if the air was charged. Buck called down "Who's there?" in a menacing tone. Castleton sprung forward in the dimly lit space, holding his gun up high over him as he raced upwards and yelled out his own greeting. "Let the girl go, Buck. Let her go nice and easy and you won't get hurt." Jake ignored the damned phone's continual ring. He moved forward with Castleton.

But when he caught sight of Belinda, his world changed. Even in the shadows, he saw Buck had a gun pointed at her head, and his hand was gripping her arm.

Without thinking, acting only on his gut-wrenching desire to do something to save her, Jake charged up past Castleton, screaming at Buck. "You heard him! Let her go! Now! It's over!"

Confused by the melee, Buck turned the gun toward Jake. As if caught in freeze-frames, the action seemed to slow. Belinda screamed. A flash of light came from Buck's gun. Something burned Jake's left arm.

He kept running forward toward Buck, grabbing at the man's legs. Buck toppled backwards on the landing. Castleton ran up and stepped on Buck's hand, grabbing his gun.

When time began again, Belinda was cowering against the wall, crying. Jake reached for her and gathered her to him with his right arm, kissing her forehead.

"It's all right, it's all right. You're safe now," he cooed to her. Something ached like the devil in his left arm.

"He was going to push me off...down the elevator shaft, like an accident—oh, my God, you're hurt!" Belinda's crying stopped as she focused on Jake. She reached over and touched his arm, letting out a soft, "oh, no" as she saw a stain on his shirt. Now, she played the comforter, making him sit on the step and lean his back against the wall. Grabbing his phone, she dialed 911.

"Oh, darling, you're shot, he shot you," she said after making the call. "Jake, I can't...oh, damn. I just love you so much. I can't lose you!" She buried her head in his shoulder, and despite the pain, Jake experienced a peace he'd not felt in months.

⊷❧

It took hours, mostly endless sessions of waiting. Waiting for the doctors. Waiting for the police. Waiting for it all to be over. But in the end, he was released with pain meds and a few stitches. The bullet only grazed him. Buck was in custody. They'd be called in to testify. Jake's theory had been right. Belinda's life insurance policy was still active, unbeknownst to her, and Buck had been trying to find the perfect "double indemnity" accident with which to cash it in.

They made it to their beach getaway, Belinda driving. And he let her flutter about him, settling him in front of a fire, giving him brandy — in lieu of pain pills — and unpacking his bags for him. When she was finished with that latter task, she returned to the condo's living room and sat beside him.

"You look like the cat that swallowed the canary," he murmured. His eyelids were closing. The brandy, the fire, the soft whoosh of waves on the shore below, the post-adrenaline release of tension all conspired against him. "I'm just so happy," she said. "Happy to be alive. Happy you're alive. Happy because…I found this." She opened her hands. There sat the ring box.

Happy she found it. There it was — a soaring favorability rating. But there was still one last question on his personal survey.

"I'd planned something more romantic than this," he said, grabbing her hands in his, wincing slightly at the movement.

When she saw his discomfort, she frowned and placed his wounded arm gently by his side. She kissed his temple, then his cheek, sweet, chaste demonstrations of affection that soon warmed both their bodies, despite all that had happened.

"This is pretty romantic, Jake," she whispered. "All I need for romance is you."

"In that case, Ms. Remington, I propose we make our lives one long romance." Using his good hand, he stroked her arm. "Will you marry me?"

"Yes," she breathed, leaning into him for a kiss with deeper meaning. "A thousand yeses," she said.

He embraced and kissed her hungrily, feeling the passion stir in him despite the hour, the pills, the energy-sapping evening. "Let's go to bed," he said huskily, "and celebrate."

"I thought you'd never ask," she murmured.

CHAPTER TWENTY-THREE

SHE HAD TYPED the last words, done the last read-through when Jim came softly into her office, knocking first on the door frame. She turned to him, smiling.

"I got a job," he announced simply.

Before she could ask about it, he continued. "It's just a small thing, working in the art department at Susquehanna Community College, a technical assistant it's called." He grinned more broadly. "You're safe...from Alice and her erotica requests."

"I didn't know you'd applied," she said in wonder.

"Didn't want to get your hopes up," he said. "Or mine." He paused. "It's Pennsylvania, but we can live in Maryland, across the river."

It was part-time, and from the description she read online after Jim told her where to find it, it sounded like glorified janitorial work, cleaning up after artists in the studio, reordering supplies. And because it was part-time, it was not enough money to support them. But did it need to be now? It was steady work. That's what she'd wanted. A steady safety net, something that would be there even if the book money wasn't. She didn't think of his art money as real. She couldn't bring herself to do that—even after the down payment had turned up in their account. At least, he'd cleaned up all those things, put that behind him. For now.

She hugged him. She suggested a celebration, but he was subdued, and so was she. It wasn't a great job, not enough to cover their expenses, and she knew he'd done it just for her, not because he had a burning desire to work at this type of thing.

When he went out to make arrangements to rent a trash bin as they started cleaning out the house for its eventual sale, she called Becky.

"Let me get this straight," Becky said after Kate told the story. "You were moaning about Jim not finding a job down here. Now he's got one, and you're moaning it's not good enough?"

"It's not enough to support us!"

"Your writing and his art sale are doing that, though, right?"

"Yes, but..."

"But what? Good Lord, Kate. You just made a dream book sale. You have another one in the works. Jim's sold some art for a pretty penny, and he still went out and landed a job because he knows you don't feel secure without a steady paycheck. Most people would say you're pretty damn successful. Have you noticed it's a jungle out there—that folks are losing their jobs, not finding new ones? For the love of God, be happy, will you? Just grab it and be happy! You don't know how lucky you are!"

Becky's voice pulsed with anger. She almost sounded on the verge of tears, in fact, so Kate backed off. She wondered if she and Bob were facing some financial challenges. She felt humbled, shamed.

"Jim stepped up," Becky continued. "Maybe you need to do the same."

"I am," Kate insisted. "I mean, I know I have to. I get it. I really do." Her insistence just made it sound as if she didn't.

As Kate backed away from whining, Becky's tone softened, and their conversation drifted to memories, with Becky suddenly eager to talk about their mother.

"You remember how you used to wear shoes until they nearly fell off your feet?" she asked Kate. "It drove Mom to despair."

"I know."

"She liked to see you looking nice. I think she felt you didn't know how pretty you were if you didn't wear nice things."

Kate smiled sadly. "Whenever I go shopping now, you know what I hear Mom whispering in my ear?"

"What?" Becky asked.

"Buy the shoes."

Becky laughed softly. "She's right, Kate. Buy the shoes. Now. Buy the shoes. Grab it."

❧❧

Two weeks later, Kate stood on a rickety pier, looking out at the Susquehanna River where it linked to the top of the Chesapeake Bay. The ground around the pier oozed mud. It was marshy and dank, overgrown and neglected. Herons glided over the water, finding refuge in tall grasses on flat spits of land. Water sparkled in the sun, a lone cloud drifted lazily, lost from its flock, amidst a blue expanse.

"The value of the land is really what you need to envision," the agent, Samantha Cummings, said, a name straight out of one of the romance novels Kate penned.

"Is the house structurally sound?" Jim asked, staring back up the hill at the building that stood there. "House" and "stood" seemed almost too extravagant to describe what they viewed. Windows covered in cardboard. Roof shingles missing, as were the steps to the front porch. The whole place needed paint. Lots of it. After a first coat of some kind of sealing oil. She wondered if it wouldn't be more cost-effective to just tear the thing down and start over.

"I can show you the engineer's report. There are some great bones here. We had an offer that fell through, and an inspection was done. Everything's in it. Nothing is hidden. Handyman's special, just like the listing says," Samantha said with a smile. She tugged at her light shrug. A breeze blew off the water, and it was chilly in the shade. They were still in the days of off-again, on-again warm weather, but its relentless approach wouldn't be denied.

But still, it smelled like spring and summer rolled into one. Dogwood bloomed in the woods. Someone was fishing in a shallow boat down river. The air felt clogged with life. Trees overhead were heavy with leaves, bright green, the insouciant color of new beginnings. When Kate closed her eyes, she saw lazy summers from her childhood, blankets spread on the lawn, books before her in the shade of a tree, or a marble notebook where she wrote story after story, tales of heroic love.

She looked at Jim. To her surprise, he didn't seem to be making for an exit. He stood, hands on his hips, squinting at the house, as if seeing how it could be, not how it was.

How it could be—she'd seen it as soon as they'd driven up. It had a porch, one that wrapped around the side of the house. It was pitted, with boards missing and posts hanging crookedly, no longer supporting the sagging roof. The floors and beams inside were not rotted, though—although they were covered with silt, blown in through poorly hanging doors and busted windows before they'd been covered with cardboard. The stair rail was off—Samantha hadn't wanted them to go upstairs, but Jim had insisted, taking the steps two at a time—and the bathrooms and kitchen all lacked fixtures. No toilet, no sinks, no stove. Those had been taken—by the previous owners or vandals.

Even so, the price was high. Any waterfront property was dear, and someone with an eye to a good investment would have snatched this up quickly if the economy had been better.

Jim had taken the lead on the house hunt. He'd seen the listing on the internet and set up the viewing. Kate wouldn't have bothered. First, it was in Pennsylvania, not Maryland. Second, the price was too much for them—she'd pictured something more modest, something they could live in for years before the writing and art money ran out. But Jim had insisted. "You wanted a white house." And Jim—Jim had wanted the waterfront, confiding how some of his best times as a kid had been fishing with his dad and brothers.

Buy the shoes.

Now he looked at Kate. They'd talked about how they'd handle a deal.

"Half of what they're asking," he said, staring Samantha in the eye. "But in cash. No waiting for mortgage papers to clear. And we'll forgo our own inspection if you give us the previous report."

Kate held her breath. Half of the asking price—that was Jim's art money plus her *Wishful Thinking* advance plus part of her advance for *The Last Romantics.* It wouldn't leave them much to live on or to work with. But Jim did have that part-time job....

"Mr. Lazlo, that's awfully low," Samantha said, still smiling.

"The house has been on the market for over a year," Jim countered. "And the longer it stays on the market, the worse it gets, making the value go lower still."

"Well, I am obligated to give every offer to the seller."

"Half. Cash," Jim repeated. "If they counter, we can't offer cash. And we'd walk away."

"All right," she said. "I'll pass it along. We'll see."

❧

They did see. The agent called them the next day, while they were having lunch with Becky in a small café in Shrewsbury, Pennsylvania.

That morning, Kate had discovered why Becky had been so sharp with her on the phone several weeks ago. And she was mortified and upset at the reason.

At the time that Kate was whining about her life, Becky had had a breast biopsy. And she'd not told Kate, not bothered her with it. But Kate had found a letter, sitting on her sister's desk crammed into a corner of their neat dining room. When she'd seen the word "biopsy" and the medical letterhead, her heart had plummeted to her stomach. But she read it, her hand trembling as she held the paper. It confirmed what a doctor had apparently told Becky by phone: all was well.

Kate had lifted the paper to her cheek, stroking it like a cat rubbing against something much loved.

No abnormality noted.

The sweetest words in the world.

No. The sweetest word was what those words meant: benign.

She'd been tender with Becky after that, helping her, not talking about herself or her woes — which now seemed miniscule — letting Becky be as involved as she wanted in their house hunt, knowing she'd enjoy it.

Becky had been spared their mother's fate, and she'd spared Kate the worry about it, too.

Now, she looked at her sister with new eyes. She had to tell her not to do that again, not to protect her like that. She wanted to be a pillar of strength to her, as Becky was to her.

"Tell me more about the deal for your book," Becky prodded. It was just like her to know that Kate liked talking about it. She happily recounted the story, even though she'd told it several times already.

"This Beatrice Rutherford person — isn't it odd she's never mentioned in any histories of the Fitzgeralds?"

"I don't think any of their servants are mentioned," Kate said, sipping at an iced coffee.

"The servants never get mentioned," Jim added. "Unless they're British."

"Then they get a Masterpiece Theater kind of show," Becky said.

It was during their laughter that Jim's phone rang.

"I know you said no counter," Samantha began, "but they're willing to come down some." Kate and Jim stepped outside, and Jim put her on speaker phone. When Samantha named the figure — twenty percent lower than the asking price — Jim cringed and shook his head. Kate nodded agreement at him.

"That's not nearly enough change for us to even consider it. No deal," he said. For a few moments, there was silence. Kate knew Samantha was waiting for them to counter, but Jim held firm. "You still there, Samantha?"

"Yes, yes. So I guess I go back and say it's over?" she asked weakly. "What about this—what about I counter with a deal that's a third lower than—"

"No deal," Jim repeated. And then he reiterated their initial terms. "You said you had another couple places to show us, right? Unless they accept what we're offering, we'll be in your office tomorrow ready to tour those other spots. I'm sure we'll find something in this market."

After he clicked off, Kate hugged him. "You did the right thing," she said.

"Did I?" he murmured into her hair.

"Hey, you two lovebirds," Becky said, coming outside. "What's the scoop? You homeowners here?"

"Not yet," Kate said and then explained.

"Half price?" Becky said quietly, eyes widening, brows lifting. They'd not told her about their offer yesterday, only that they'd looked at a run-down riverfront property.

"We can't afford any more than that," Jim said.

"It's a stretch, as is," Kate said. "I feel bad for the owners, but at least it's something, and they probably paid it off years ago."

"Moot point," Jim said. "They won't let it go now. So they'll keep paying taxes and the rest on it while the house rots to the ground."

"Ouch. It was in that bad shape?" Becky asked. They'd described it to her and Bob, but not in gory detail.

"Pretty bad," said Kate, now thinking that perhaps this was a sign they shouldn't get this house, that it was too much to pay and too much to do. What if her writing didn't continue to pull in money? Jim's part-time job wouldn't pay the mortgage. They were better off looking for something far more modest and less work.

"Tomorrow's another day," Jim said flatly.

CHAPTER TWENTY-FOUR

BUT BY TOMORROW, they were the owners—at least on paper—of the run-down house. The sellers relented to a figure very close to what they'd offered, but just enough over it to save face, taking the bird offered from their hands. Preliminary papers were signed, champagne flutes clinked at Becky and Bob's and they were on their way back to Vermont.

She couldn't write. There was too much to do. For the first time in a long time, she started living...instead of writing about living.

And now, in what seemed a reverse of the Litany of Events that had led them here, good things happened one after the other. Before their first open house in Vermont, their agent told them she had interest. The house was so reasonably priced—it was small, close to town, a good "starter home" — that their agent knew the perfect couple. They came and saw the place and put in an offer. Kate and Jim still held the open house, but when no interest materialized immediately after that, they accepted the young couple's bid after countering with a reasonable amount, which was countered by a number that had them meeting in the middle. The quick sale meant they wouldn't need to use her *Wishful Thinking* advance for the home in Maryland, after all.

"We can use it for the renovation," Jim said.

So they packed and cleaned and laughed and partied. They had a couple farewell bashes, including a surprise one thrown by Keith and Pat. They enjoyed their last summer in Vermont, the best season it had to offer. No need for air conditioning. Cool nights, warm days, that green glow on the mountains, air fresh as new snow but warm as a baby's breath.

Not once did Jim express regret about moving from this, even though she saw a wistful look come into his eye in the evening when they sat on their patio, on the steps to the kitchen. Instead, he talked about his plans for their new house, how he was speaking with contractors—recommended by Bob—about getting the kitchen and upstairs bath outfitted, and one bedroom habitable.

"That way, we can live there while I work on it," he said. "It'll be a bitch, but it'll save us a heap of cash not to have to rent somewhere."

"We could stay with Becky. She's offered," Kate said.

"I know. That's our fallback."

But she, too, wanted to be in their own place.

They settled at the end of the month in Vermont, then piled their car high with belongings the movers hadn't taken, and drove down to Pennsylvania where they settled on the new house the next day.

During the drive, Kate came to a conclusion. She knew how to finish Beatrice Rutherford's story. The book had sold based on the vision of an alternative ending to the Fitzgerald drama, a more satisfying denouement to their requited love. Kate knew how to write that story in spades. She knew happily-ever-afters like the back of her hand. And she'd at last be able to write a real one, not a sugar-coated finish with nary a reference to clouds on the horizon. She'd be able to write a real ending, where people who loved each other struggled and fought and wrestled with each other and life and finally came to realize that all that mattered, really, was how they'd loved one another...and themselves.

CHAPTER TWENTY-FIVE

THE MARCH OF TIME by Beatrice Rutherford
People thought she died in that fire. The truth's different, and the world needs to know. It's a story of redemption, of the small footsteps turning away from the bad and toward the good. It's about plodding toward the light, not galloping. And that's so much of what life is anyway. Sometimes I just want to shout it to everyone, to stop looking for the dramatic moment and the big ideas. Listen to the small voice and go about getting things done and treating each other with tenderness.

I think two things helped her. One was medicine. The doctors seemed to have hit on some drug that gave her peace, that calmed her spirits enough for her to wrest control from her demons. It was by accident she learned how to do this. They forgot a dosage for a few days, and on those days as she came out of the stupor of the drug, she was alert. Alert enough to live.

The second thing that helped her was...me. Well, not me coming up with a plan or directing her toward relief. No, it was her helping me that helped her, if you can follow that.

I must admit to a bit of breakdown myself, you see. Scott had been unkind to me, as I reported. And he was going off to Hollywood. And I'd been typing *Tender,* getting angrier and angrier at how long it was taking him, how he was using Zelda's pain, how he wasn't using his best talents. And Jeremy had been haunting my thoughts something fierce. That's when I heard him loudest telling me not to judge, just as I was at the pinnacle of my scathing critiques of those around me. So I'd done a foolish thing and started turning the light of judgment on myself. That can lower a man, for sure, and it had brought me to my knees as I'd seen how I'd wasted many a year tied to this self-centered pair when I could have been out there with all the other little red hens, making a way for myself. I was afraid for my future, what would happen if I didn't have a job. Times were bad.

And in the middle of a visit with her, on one of those days she was awakening, I got annoyed with Zelda as she complained about Scott. Now, mind you, I thought Scott had used his wife in his art to a shockingly selfish degree. I commiserated with Zelda thinking Scott's anger at her own writing was unfair. But when she set to whining about something being wrong with her room—can't remember what now—and how she wished Scott would just put her in a public place and be done with it, I'd had enough of both of them.

Trembling, I stood before her, wagging my finger with all the sanctimonious rage in my bosom, and I told her to be grateful for a man who loved her so much he was sacrificing his very life, second by second, moment by moment, day by day, for her well being. If that's not love, then what is, I shouted at her. And having a man love you like that—having anyone love you like that—is the greatest thing on God's earth. It was the very love of God himself, I yelled.

And I wept. Wept so hard, I can't remember much about it except that I was in a stupor myself, as if her madness was contagious and I'd caught a touch of it.

She sat silent, I remember that, and I figured she was sinking back into one of her states. But at some point, she got up and came to me, putting her arm around me, leading me to the bed, setting me down, patting me, stroking my hair.

"There, there, Bea," she said. "You are so good to us, so good and true. We should take better care of you."

Better care of me. I do believe that was the moment on her road to Damascus when the light hit her. When she stopped searching for the things that made her feel better and started looking for the things that would make me—and him—feel better. That became her impetus.

She struggled mightily over the weeks that followed, looking for just the right dosage of the drug to keep her mental state somewhat balanced. She'd surreptitiously throw away some, she confided to me, and asked me to take notes on how much she was taking and what got her to the right place.

I leapt to this assignment. Excited, I came every chance I could with my notebook and pen. We were conspirators, out to overthrow the tyranny of insanity. And in the end, we did, wrestling just enough cool-headedness from the regimen to give her what she needed to survive. She had good days and bad, but she learned on the bad ones to lock herself away, to lie down and wait it out, to take a little more medicine if needed. She fought, really fought for her equilibrium. How I admired that slow, quiet battle, accomplished with no fanfare.

Scott saw some of it happen before he left, but he was skeptical, and I don't blame him. She'd gotten better and relapsed before. Neither she nor I judged him harshly for his doubts. Eventually, she and I took off for her mother's home down south, Scott earnestly telling me to look after her. But I could see in his eyes the relief of letting go of his burden for a while.

As for me, I wondered how I'd feel settling in again in my beloved south. It filled me with peace, every clacking mile down the track. I felt like kissing the ground when we arrived, but I was grateful for the bustle of moving in to distract me from memories and regret.

As Zelda improved, Scott was off in Hollywood earning money to pay for all her treatments. He was also betraying us both, as history showed. He'd promised to send me drafts of his next book to type, but I only got little pieces here and there, and I must say it excited me because it was feeling a lot like *Gatsby* to me, with that sense of longing and bittersweet regret laced through it, but with an overlay of maturity and wisdom now that only the passing of years bestows. But it turns out he was having someone out there type up most of it, so he was cheating on me, in a small way, giving away the first read of his beauteous words to some stranger.

Oh, the bigger betrayal is one the ages now record, his affair with that gossip columnist. I shall not name her. Even Zelda got wind of it through a friend of a friend. Some friend, say I. You don't go breaking a heart for no good reason.

And she was broken up about it, so much so that I feared she'd go into decline once again. Her mother was no help in that regard. Her mother thought Scott never good enough for her, that he'd soiled her, that he'd somehow led her down perdition's path. She fed Zelda a load full of those judgments.

Zelda sobbed away a good number of nights, and her momma even talked about taking her back to the sanitarium. No, I said, putting my foot down. She's got a right to be unhappy at unhappy news. Give her time.

So we did. And she didn't drift into that mesmerized state or the other one, the wild one where she wanted to do everything at that one moment. She stayed calm. A steely look came in her eye. She told me she was going to write Scott, tell him she understood his straying, thanking him for all he'd done for her, telling him she required little else but the knowledge he'd loved her once, that she'd not stand in his way. The meaning was clear—she was giving him permission to leave her, to divorce her. It was a beautiful letter—she asked me to read it before sending it—filled with the purest kind of love, the love of letting go that which you love the most, placing your Isaac on the altar.

He came home.

What a visit, on a hot day where stepping outside put a sheen of sweat on your face even in the early hours! The crickets were hissing out the end of summer, such a racket you could hardly hear the babble of a fountain nearby, where everything felt still and authentic.

They went to sit out under the magnolia trees near the fountain with its cooling burbles. Zelda told her momma to go run her errands. She insisted on it, fairly pushed her out of the house. I was allowed to stay, and I confess to eavesdropping, pretending to wash dishes and such in the kitchen, but peering out to the bright green yard beyond, to the deep shade and the glistening water.

She did most of the talking. She asked him how things were going, and she told him how she was doing. I knew he was wary. I'd seen it in his eyes. And I didn't blame him none. Zelda had been through ups and downs when we'd thought she was cured before. How was he to know this was a steadier calm, a smoother place?

I knew she was nervous — she'd confided in me that she was afraid Scott wouldn't like this person she'd become, that she knew he'd fallen in love with someone she wasn't — couldn't — be anymore. And then she'd said, before I could even counsel or comfort, that she'd just have to face that. The truth was better than wondering.

I heard her voice trembling a little as she spoke, and that made me nervous, thinking he might interpret that as a sign she still wasn't stable. But her voice was so low and …right. Filled with a bright honesty that just took your breath away to hear.

She said how grateful she was to all the "treasure" he'd heaped on her, how she knew that paying all her doctor bills had been a strain. And truth to tell, he did look pale and unwell, as if the weight of the world was on him. She placed her hand on his as they sat, side by side, on a wooden bench, and she said she'd never be able to repay him except with peace of mind.

I saw the question in his eyes when he turned to her, but she kept on talking.

"It's understandable, Scott, that we might find it hard to be true to the people we once thought we were."

My, what a pretty, soft way to put it — *true to the people we once thought we were.* They'd both thought they were the brightest, most modern, most youthful people living at any given moment. And that had been their appeal. They were the moment.

But she was really telling him with those words that she wasn't who she'd been, and she couldn't be that girl anymore, even if she were willing to try. And she was also telling him it was all right if he'd strayed, as long as he came back. But if he didn't want to be with the girl she'd become, she'd go on and love him and be grateful to him all the same as he went away.

He crumpled to the ground, and my breath caught. I started to head to the door, thinking he'd collapsed and a doctor was needed.

But, no. Instead, he knelt before her. He gazed into her eyes, his own shining. And then he placed his head in her lap and wept.

She stroked his head, saying "hush, now, everything's going to be all right. Hush, now, my love. Let me take care of you."

And I cried too, silent, in the kitchen door. I can't write any more about it. It was too powerful for words.

୶ஒஒ

Scott had to go back to Hollywood, of course, to finish his work. But the time he stayed in Alabama was the sweetest of their married lives, I think. Zelda sent her mother and me both packing, so they could have the little house to themselves. I went off to visit a cousin of Jeremy's, a kind enough woman with whom I had little in common save our thin connection of family now past. When I returned a week later, Scott was gone, back to California.

He wrote Zelda constantly and called her at least once a week, expense be damned. And they were planning on living together again, maybe in Alabama, maybe Georgia, but not New York, not Europe, not anywhere near the old, bad influences that seemed to force them to take on different personages, roles they felt compelled to play. Zelda was planning for this new life like a new bride, even putting together a trousseau of sorts that I helped her sew — pretty new undergarments and embroidered pillowcases, even a tablecloth and some fine linen napkins. Her mother didn't approve, but her clucking didn't stop Zelda from being happy and moving on with her plans.

It was a different kind of happy, too. There was a serenity about it. It made me realize she was cured for sure.

But then we all know what happened. He died. He dropped dead out there, in that woman's apartment, even though he'd said he'd ended it with her. Oh, I think he had. I like to believe he had. And he'd gone over that one day to sort out some business with her, maybe gather the papers for his novel that stranger was typing – maybe it was her.

When Zelda got word, she sat down on the edge of her bed and just stared. I thought for sure this was the beginning of another episode, of another madness. And that view seemed true when she hardly ate or drank or spoke for the next few days. It was near the holidays, too, when everyone's cheer just made your own heartbreak all the worse. I knew that territory.

But I knew she was all right when she told her momma one day to stop hovering over her. And then Zelda took me aside and told me her plan.

"Bea," she said. "I have my life back. Not something people think is my life from what he wrote about it. Just my life. A new one that's just mine." And I could see that she'd given herself permission to grab this consolation, this ability to take back what had once been only hers before Scott had come into her life. It wasn't that she didn't still love Scott or mourn him, but it was as though his death was a final gift to her, a "go in peace" blessing. It draped over her like gossamer, making her bright and new.

She asked me if I'd come with her, if I'd help her. She said she couldn't afford to pay me much, but she had a mind to do more writing, and she knew how much I'd helped out with Scott's papers.

My prospects were slim. The country wasn't exactly jumping with possibilities at that time. And war clouds were darkening Europe. Even if I'd wanted to walk away — which I didn't want to do — I couldn't.

So I said, yes, knowing I'd be making little more than room and board.

She'd gotten it into her head that she'd never be free of Scott's vision of her, though, even though he himself was gone. She believed everyone would look for her to carry his torch or such like, keeping the flame of his brilliance alive. And she believed that would just kill her, to have to be the girl he wrote about, the girl he'd preserved in the warm amber of his stories.

So, she set about hatching a plot that would have never made it past an editor had he written it down. She enlisted few, taking only three of us into her confidence — her mother, Scottie, and me.

The end of this story has never been told, but here it is:

Zelda got her momma to go along with a tall tale that she'd been hospitalized again, even going so far as to record her name at an institution as if she were being forced to go in. But she escaped — yes, she actually climbed out a window and ran to my waiting car in the dead of night, us both giggling like schoolgirls on the lam.

The next day, she called the place pretending to be her mother and asking for herself. When they couldn't produce "Zelda," she went into high dudgeon, claiming she'd call the authorities on them for their shoddy safety, and if they let out one word about her "poor baby" being on the loose, she'd personally sue the doctor in charge for breach of contract or something. It was a great performance, and I could tell she enjoyed giving it, almost too much.

Well, after that, they weren't going to say a peep. They just hushed it up, and everyone thought Zelda Fitzgerald was in some sanitarium, poor child, living out her life in grief and despair.

But instead, she and I took off for the hills of Texas. She'd planned it out well enough. She had located a town that was big enough to hide in but small enough to handle. Paradise Hill. She took back her name – Sayre, that is—and called herself Zinnia. She did love flowers and was partial, too, to the singularity of a name beginning with the last letter of the alphabet.

Zinnia Sayre—it was a mouthful. But she blossomed, just like her new name, with that moniker. She opened a dance studio and taught little girls how to pirouette and point their toes. She did write, though not as much as she might have intended, and I ended up tending the house more than typing up her notes. Mostly, she wrote long letters to Scottie, forcing her to promise to burn them after she read them, like she was some spy. She saw Scottie, too, but her daughter's visits weren't numerous. Traveling then wasn't as easy as it got to be, and, like all adult children, Scottie started in on living her own life. She kept her mother's secret, maybe fearing a slip back into the madness that had previously bedeviled her. One was tender around those who'd been claimed by such illnesses of the mind, never knowing what would set them off. And I dare say that Zelda sometimes did play with that notion, blurting out what might have seemed like inappropriate remarks at times but what was really just honesty in its bare-bones form.

She lived a good life, though we were both broken-hearted with war coming on, seeing sons and husbands go off and not come back. My, she was a comfort to me then as I was taken back to memories of losing Jeremy. How hard it was to see the mothers mourn, and it put me to remembering how I'd not reached out nearly enough to Jeremy's family after he'd passed.

And, after the war, there was news, of course, of that awful fire at the sanitarium where she was supposed to be lodged. Oh, for a few days we were in a daze over that, what she'd blessedly missed. She managed to get out the word, though, that she'd "died" in that conflagration. She even had a funeral and memorial put together.

I think that took the last worry from her shoulders and let her breathe free and clear. She no longer worried about some intrepid reporter finding her or some town resident remarking on her resemblance to an old photo of F. Scott's wife. Now she could chuckle honestly and say, "yes, I've heard that before," not fretting that the thought might turn into an investigation of who she really was.

Zinnia Sayre passed away quietly in 1968, too soon if you asked me. She was alive and laughing at the barre in her little studio — even at that age, she was still spry — when she suddenly dropped, felled by a massive stroke, the doctor said, gone in a flash.

As for me, I'm writing these notes on the cool front porch of my little white farmhouse tucked away in the countryside of Maryland, not far from that ill-named La Paix estate. Zinnia — Zelda, that is — saw to my "retirement," the dear thing, including money in her will enough for me to purchase this old place. It reminded me of the house I grew up in down in Alabama, the one where I knew happiness and the lightness of heart that is never recovered once you've tasted sorrow. In it, I sometimes imagine Jeremy is going to come through the door, and more than once I've awakened from a nap thinking I see his shadow gliding up the walk, that particular open lope of his, his hat already in his hand out of respect. I see him in his uniform sometimes, too, and I think I hear him whistle and then say, soft as the breeze, "I told you I'd fetch you, Bea. You haven't been waiting long, now, have you?"

CHAPTER TWENTY-SIX

COFFEE. MMM. SHE smelled it. She pulled back the sheet and rubbed her eyes. Then she carefully slid into her slippers. No walking barefoot in this house until all the work was done. As careful as they'd been to sweep up the bedroom and hallway, stray splinters and nails were everywhere. Today she was going to vacuum, wearing a dust mask while she worked.

Light shone everywhere, a shadow-dappled light of moving images, the branches from the trees swaying in the wind. They were lucky. It was cool. Hot spells could last into October here. Poor Jim—how he'd loved the cold of Vermont, and they'd moved during the state's best season into the end of this one's worst. And they'd not put in air-conditioning until the rest of the house was done. So, they'd experience the swampy heat of the tidal region, with its sticky nights, its mosquito-infested evenings. She looked forward to it.

"Morning," she said to Jim in the kitchen, as she ambled over to the coffeemaker. He'd put out the croissants they'd bought the night before for their first breakfast in the house. They were on one of her pretty yellow plates, a napkin covering them. When she turned to thank him, she noticed him bent over the table, drawings spread before him.

Meticulous drawings done to scale on graph paper.

"What's that?" she asked, coming closer.

"Some stuff I put together. This is the living room," he said, pointing, "and it can open to the dining room here, if we knock out this wall and put in another to separate it from the kitchen. Then we make the kitchen bigger by knocking out the mudroom wall — don't worry, we have that here, off the side, by the breezeway to the garage...."

She heard him talking, but her mind focused on an epiphany springing from the pages. His rendering was neat and beautiful, straight lines and fluffy curves to represent shrubbery. It looked like something done by a professional.

Jim could draw, really draw. He did have talent. And it was something he'd loved to do. He loved this. This was his art. And she'd mocked him for it. She'd been the snob!

He'd hidden his passion from her, perhaps afraid what she might think. And she'd tried to destroy it. But he'd done precisely what she had done at first with her writing — choosing an art form she thought suitable for her pedigree, something simple and easy to appreciate. And he'd been relentlessly self-deprecating about his creations, never making them into more than they were. That way he'd be safe from real judgment — just as she'd done, with her romance writing. Oh, God. Would he ever forgive her? Could she convince him to take it up again?

She remembered a conversation she'd had with Becky just this past week. Always Kate's most useful critic, Becky had read *Wishful Thinking* in manuscript form. She'd liked it a great deal, pointing out a few things here and there she thought could be improved. She didn't mind the story's heat, and thought Kate had handled it well. Then, she'd looked at Kate and said, "You used Jim to model Jake, didn't you?"

Kate had been flabbergasted. "What? Jim? Jake is sophisticated, wealthy, and doesn't look a thing like Jim. Plus, I gave him a British accent."

Becky had peered at her over reading glasses in her bright kitchen. "First off, we've had the sophisticated talk already, and you know how I feel about that. You might have been raised in a Tim McGraw household, but you have a Mozart heart when it comes to writing...."

"Yeah, yeah, yeah."

"Stop it. It's tiresome. Listen up: Belinda is you. All your heroines are you. I've told you that before. You, struggling to be independent, to be taken seriously. Belinda comes from our background—not the abusive stepdad and all, but the working-class mores, the grandchildren of immigrants past. But Belinda is self-confident—how you long to be! And she longs to be loved and protected, too. As for Jim...just like Jake, he's not conventionally handsome. He's taciturn, has trouble expressing himself to you because he's always wondering what's the right thing, what you want...and he's superprotective. Remember that section when Jake's in town and Belinda has to stay late at work? And she's thinking of all the reasons she loves Jake? That's you. Talking about Jim."

Becky had said more, too, telling her that the Rutherford story was also to an extent Kate's, Kate longing to find the big romantic gesture in the small steps of life and love. "You need to stop and—" Kate had shushed her at that, laughing. "Please, no clichés," she'd said. But in her heart, she wondered if such clichés took root because they were so true.

Kate thought about the scene in *Wishful Thinking*, Belinda at her desk writing down the pros and cons of staying with Jake, and how the pros list had been long and detailed, the con list only holding the single phrase: "annoying things." Annoying things, just like the irritations of everyday life, the little rubbing up against one another that was sometimes rough, sometimes gentle, but always a reminder you weren't alone—even when you wanted to be alone. Unavoidable in any human contact.

Becky had plowed on. "You think Jim's not like Jake? He took you to Vermont when you were a nervous wreck. He's always looking out for you. He even got a job here, remember? A job, I might add, he doesn't really need to hold. He did it just for you, Kate. *Just for you*. It's like he took the bullet for you—the one Jake took for Belinda. He'd do anything to make you happy. I can't believe you didn't think of him when you wrote Jake."

She couldn't believe it either. Despite her lighthearted attitude when Becky had made her observations, Kate was shaken by them. They upended her view of herself, of Jim. Yes, she loved Jim. Like most marriages, theirs had evolved from first-blush passion to steady warmth. No one had ever tempted her. If anything, when she'd wondered if she and Jim would make it, she'd envisioned herself alone after a breakup. Her breath caught at that thought. Life without Jim—it was unbearable to contemplate now. Jim was always there for her, a cheerleader, a booster, a believer in her talent.

Becky was right. Jim was every hero in her books, just dressed in different clothing, different personality quirks. But deep down, they were all Jim—loving, tender, protective. In her books, she made his traits heroic, bigger, writ large. In real life, she'd found some of them exasperating, irritating, the rough edges of life itself. *Life isn't a novel or a movie,* she whispered to herself. Jim was no storybook hero, and she was no heroine. They were both flawed individuals doing the best they could. But he loved her unconditionally. Shouldn't she do the same? What did she fear?

Jim didn't have to start his new job until next Monday, but now she thought she'd tell him to bag that, to work on his own art while she pursued hers. And if the money ran out, they'd both get jobs—at McDonald's if they had to. She couldn't keep waiting for some wand to be waved. If she wanted to write her kinds of stories, she'd write them. Like Belinda, she needed to be independent, striking out on her own. If her only readers were Becky, Jim, Marie, Jackie and maybe her nieces, she'd still write these stories. And she'd find something else to support themselves with.

She looked around her. As he talked, she saw it all. The bright, open living and dining room, the cheery kitchen with the big white cupboard that would fit in perfectly here, the gardens on the side, the half bath, the laundry room, the mudroom near the garage, her office—he'd made sure there was room for her office— on the back looking out into the woods, with one window catching a glimpse of water below....he'd thought of it all.

One more year and you'll be happy...

One more year, and she was happy. When Jim played that music, had he been thinking of her, wishing she'd be happy just with him? Had his happiness been complete all along?

She put her coffeecup down and hugged him. She kissed him exuberantly, passionately.

"I love you," she said.

As he embraced her, her gaze lifted to the window. Outside, the trees swayed, and in the distance, a shimmering blur of water glistened, the river sparkling silver in morning sun. There was a pier across the way, in Maryland, the state where she'd wanted to settle, with another house up on a hill. She had no yearning to be there. She was home. She resolved to place a green light at the end of their own little dock.

EPILOGUE

THE LAST ROMANTICS BY KATHERINE BRZNECKI
Most of all, I wanted them to be happy. She never stopped loving Scott—kept his picture and copies of all his books near her bed at all times. She never entertained the thought of another romance, even though there were suitors—she was a good-looking woman again once the madness lifted.

And I like to think of them together now, in a mystic sweet communion, in a place where the ravages of ego and self are gone, and all that's left is the pure shimmering essence of their great romantic love, distilled to the crystals of what was best about both of them—not the fireworks and champagne days of their youthful ardor, not the passion and physical needs that pulled them like celestial bodies toward each other, but the harder work that came later, the love that had to be proven and refined, that had to wait in the shadows while storms passed, that had to believe. And sacrifice more than they ever would have imagined in those carefree days when laughter was their currency and liquor their inspiration.

We all wanted them to be happy, didn't we? And now, we can believe they are.

A NOTE TO READERS

Any writer who's been in this business for more than a few years will probably nod her head at some of the fictional scenarios involving Kate, the romance writer, her agent and editor experiences, and those of her writing friends. Several of the rejection letters Kate receives are based on rejections my writing friends and I have seen. Some writers might even recognize ones they've gotten, as well.

I will readily admit that my writing career, such as it is, has not been anywhere near as successful as Kate's, despite her complaints to the contrary. I've always used writing income to supplement steadier cash streams, not supplant them. And I've never come close to having a best-seller. Nonetheless, like Kate, I can't seem to give up telling stories, and I feel fortunate to live in a time where self-publishing has become far easier, so those of us with stories that stray from publishing's tried-and-true can still have our voices heard.

How much of Kate's writing life is complete fiction or fact-based remains sealed in the vault of storytelling. I will only suggest that Stephen King's definition of good fiction – that it is the truth within the lie – surely has significance in her and her friends' tales. And I will 'fess up to trying to capture the many silly exchanges I've had with several published writer friends about the business.

My goal wasn't to denigrate those who work in publishing; neither, however, was I keen on sugar-coating some of the recurring challenges of the business. But I did want to pull the veil back just a little on an industry that is part art, part pure entertainment, part business, part fakery, with lots of sophistication and snobbery thrown in as the icing on top!

Kate's story wasn't even the hen that hatched this book. It was Beatrice Rutherford and her voice, whispering in my ear: *Most of all, I wanted them to be happy.*

I've never gone through a course of study of literary analysis of the Fitzgerald oeuvres. I just read them. Virtually all of them, as far as I can tell, from the short stories to *The Last Tycoon*, including the musty *The Crack-up* and Zelda's own *Save Me the Waltz*. I've read Nancy Milford's wonderful biography of Zelda, and I know I've devoured a few of Scott, too, but the titles and authors escape me, lost in the mists of time.

Recently, after rereading the Milford work, Beatrice's phrase echoed in my heart: *Most of all, I wanted them to be happy.*

Scott and Zelda, that is. Oh, if only they could have been! They had the elements of a great love—strong loyalty, despite several incidents of straying, enormous sacrifice, the willingness to be bound to each other in the most horrible of circumstances. In sickness and in health...they stayed together through the sickness part, that's for sure, Scott insisting on paying for the more expensive private institutions that housed Zelda when she pleaded with him to save money by placing her in public ones.

And, as my Beatrice points out, Scott never betrayed Zelda in print. Unlike other famous authors who avenged themselves on lovers and cast-aside spouses with scurrilous verbal portraits of their past amours, Scott painted his great love as a beauty until the very end of his days, well beyond when she was as attractive in the very real world. Due to Scott, Zelda will always be remembered as the alluring Daisy Buchanan, the attractive Nicole Diver, the fetching heroines of dozens of short stories.... He stayed true in his own way.

So, this great love affair had a happy ending of sorts, despite the ghastly denouements they both faced. They stayed true until the end. Why couldn't they have found happiness in that fidelity in life?

That was the impetus for this story, trying to envision how an HEA—happily ever after—would have manifested itself for them. It wouldn't have been in cloying embraces and promises of days of bliss to come. It would have been in serenity and acceptance.

But as I wrote this story, I was drawn to telling more than one tale. To tell only theirs would have been, it seemed to me, too clever by half, the straying from reality a large leap of faith for readers to take with me, a leap perhaps into the fantasy genre, not general fiction. So I built a bridge to that new reality by grounding my Beatrice in the here and now with troubled Kate. Kate struggled, too, with her own HEAs—those she had to write to satisfy her editor and the one she wrestled with in her own marriage.

So, in the end, this book became a treatise on requited love. Kate loves her husband, Jim, but struggles with the "march of time," the big and small challenges all couples face. Her frustration with him mirrors, to some degree, her frustration with her career. She unknowingly glamorizes Jim, though, in her romance hero, Jake, taking the best parts of her husband—his protectiveness, his care, his steadfast loyalty and support—and pasting them on her romance hero.

So this book is also about the relentless journey of requited love, its disappointments, its fears, its hopes...and how Kate, the heroine of this book, learns to accept the beauty of knowing that the love she chose long ago is still the love she needs as days "beat on...against the current..." ceaselessly into her future.

Elizabeth Malin
Fall 2015